The Wills Creek Chronicles

THE WILLS CREEK CHRONICLES

A COLLECTION OF FICTIONAL SHORT STORIES BY THE CAMBRIDGE WRITERS WORKSHOP

RAINY DAY PUBLISHING
CAMBRIDGE, OHIO

The Wills Creek Chronicles
ISBN 978-0-615-33207-9

The Wills Creek Chronicles. Copyright © 2009, Rainy Day Publishing, Cambridge, Ohio. Printed and bound in the United States of America. All rights reserved. No part of this book may be used or reproduced in any manner whatsoever – except by a reviewer who may quote brief passages in a review – without written permission from the publisher.

RAINY DAY PUBLISHING
CAMBRIDGE, OHIO

CONTENTS

Preface .... *vii*

Foreword...................................... *viii*

BEVERLY J. JUSTICE — *Junk in Harry's Closet*.................. *1*

SAMUEL D. BESKET — *Strange Encounter*......................... *3*

JOY WILBERT-ERSKINE — *The Spitting Champion*.................. *7*

BARBARA KERNODLE-ALLEN — *Granny's Revenge* *9*

RICHARD A. DAIR — *Jimmy-Joe's First Love*............... *12*

DICK METHENY — *Who Killed Sheryl?* *15*

DONA McCONNELL — *All A Mule Can Do*...................... *20*

MARALYN COOPER O'CONNELL — *A Bouquet of Limericks* *25*

MARILYN DURR — *The Body On The Dock* *27*

PAM RITCHEY — *The Letter* *29*

J. PAULETTE FORSHEY — *Uncle Eugene* *31*

LINDA BURRIS — *Pa And Ma Go To Town*............. *33*

DONNA WELLS — *The Witch of Wills Creek* *36*

DONNA J. LAKE SHAFER — *J.P.'s Model "A" Ford*................. *40*

LINDA WARRICK — *Life In The Cemetery*................... *42*

BEVERLY J. JUSTICE — *Art For Art's Sake* *46*

SAMUEL D. BESKET — *Alex The Ax*................................ *49*

MARILYN DURR — *Broiling Encounter* *52*

RICHARD A. DAIR — *The Last Straw* *57*

DICK METHENY — *Love At First Sight*............................. *60*

DONA McCONNELL — *Lion's Share* *63*

JERRY WOLFROM — *Autumn of 1945*............................ *68*

RICHARD A. DAIR — *A Woman of Courage*.................. *71*

JOY L. WILBERT-ERSKINE — *The Dead Girl Next Door* *75*

BEVERLY J. JUSTICE — *The Good Book* *80*

BARBARA KERNODLE-ALLEN	*Was It Fred's Plan?*	*83*
J. PAULETTE FORSHEY	*Mr. Lambert's Library*	*86*
SAMUEL D.BESKET	*Final Meeting*	*90*
DICK METHENEY	*Is Mike Regan Dead or Alive?*	*92*
LINDA BURRIS	*Hermit of Wills Creek*	*96*
JOETTA VARANASI	*Tipple Over The Creek*	*99*
JOY L. WILBERT-ERSKINE	*Chances*	*102*
DONNA J. LAKE SHAFER	*Joe And The Competition*	*104*
JERRY WOLFROM	*Bulldog Cleaned Up The Town*	*108*
BEVERLY J. JUSTICE	*Mystery of Sutler's Pond*	*110*
BARBARA KERNODLE-ALLEN	*Hunting Firsts*	*114*
PAM RITCHEY	*Dust And Dreams*	*116*
JERRY WOLFROM	*Kissing In The Moonlight*	*118*
J. PAULETTE FORSHEY	*Estate of Thaddeus P. Lambert*	*120*
DICK METHENEY	*Serial Killer On The Loose*	*126*
JOY L. WILBERT-ERSKINE	*Familiar Trappings*	*131*
DONNA J. LAKE SHAFER	*An Offer We Refused*	*134*
JOETTA VARANASI	*Longhorn Meets The Settlers*	*138*
PAM RITCHEY	*Lights Out*	*141*
DONA McCONNELL	*Maggie's Lesson*	*143*
LINDA BURRIS	*Wills Creek Wedding*	*148*
SAMUEL D. BESKET	*The Embezzler*	*151*
MARILYN DURR	*Needed: One Good Driver*	*156*
JERRY WOLFROM	*The Echo of Little Kate*	*160*
RICHARD A. DAIR	*Crazy Sally*	*166*
LINDA WARRICK	*One Special Friend*	*170*
DONNA J. LAKE SHAFER	*Uncle Jim Takes The Plunge*	*173*
LINDA BURRIS	*Tale of Two Weddings*	*175*
JOETTA VARANASI	*Neighborhood Excitement*	*177*
JANET MONTE	*Life Changes Forever*	*179*
	About the Authors	*183*

PREFACE

In January 2008 some 34 residents from all corners of Guernsey County, Ohio, came together for an organizational meeting. There are now 20 active writers who have made amazing advances as they pursue such writing interests as mainstream fiction, horror, romance, fantasy, the occult, humor, crime, mysteries, history and life experiences in both short story and novel form.

"The Wills Creek Chronicles" is a joint effort by members to provide readers with short, interesting fictional stories. We appreciate the Crossroads Library and Christ United Methodist Church for providing us with a meeting room, Mike Neilson, *The Daily Jeffersonian*, for the cover photography, and member Rick Dair, who took our individual photos.

We've enjoyed writing this book and willingly acknowledge that any misspellings or typographical errors are our own.

Jerry Wolfrom
Instructor

MISSION STATEMENT

The Cambridge Writers Workshop is an unofficial, not-for-profit organization established to provide an environment designed to educate local writers, encourage them to continue writing, expand their literary horizons and enhance their creative abilities in order to broaden their future choices in the publication of their own works.

FORWARD

A Few Notes About Wills Creek

Wills Creek is a twisting, almost nondescript little waterway meandering aimlessly from Southeastern Guernsey County, Ohio, to the northwest corner, where it crosses into Coshocton County. There's nothing special about the creek, except that it can be swollen, angry and ugly at times, and picturesque at others. Note, however, that it provides water to several areas in several parts of the county.

Some 200 years ago local Indians called "Wills Creek," then much wider and deeper, "The Mad River" because it flows from south to north. At one time in history small paddle-wheelers negotiated the waters.

When members of the Cambridge (Ohio) Writers Workshop looked for a common theme to tie their creative short stories together, they selected Wills Creek. In this book writers have fictionalized many locations and characters. The result is a collection of stories, both long and short, using the creek as a backdrop.

BEVERLY J. JUSTICE

Junk in Harry's Closet
One Man's Junk Is Another Man's Fortune

"For heaven's sake, Harry, get rid of this junk!" Joan lamented as she pulled a sweater from the bedroom closet. "The top shelf is bowing in the middle and could break at any time."

"It's not junk," Harry replied meekly.

Joan's complaints about the closet had dwindled in the past few weeks, perhaps because she realized that her nagging would never stir Harry to discard his accumulated treasures. Somewhere in the four boxes of baseball cards was one of Pete Rose as a rookie. Who else this side of Wills Creek could claim to own one of those? And the four boxes of comic books were a prize any serious collector would envy. Why couldn't Joan see how much they meant to him? He couldn't store them in the basement or garage as the moisture would destroy them.

"I'm leaving now," said Joan as she hurried to the door. "See you at nine."

Harry loved Thursday nights. Joan had church choir practice for two hours on Thursdays. Two hours of peace and quiet!

He got a plate of tuna casserole Joan had made and plopped himself in front of the TV. Just as he placed his feet upon the footstool he saw the shadow of something behind him.

"Don't do anything stupid, buster!"

The voice was gruff and unfamiliar. Harry looked up to see a man dressed in black, complete with a black ski mask. He was pointing a handgun at Harry. Harry's plate slipped from his hands, spilling the casserole down the front of his pants. He was paralyzed except for his bladder, which added its contents to the casserole mess on his pants.

"Where do you keep your money?" demanded the intruder.

"We-we-we d-don't have much, but it's in a safe in the bedroom," Harry managed to say.

"Then get off your butt and let's go!"

"Yes, sir; yes, sir."

The robber followed Harry to the bedroom. Harry opened the closet door to reveal a small metal safe on the floor.

"Open it!" the robber shouted, gesturing with the gun.

Harry removed a ring of keys from his pocket and selected a key with a green plastic cover.

"Hurry up! I don't have all night!"

Harry jumped at the man's voice. He knelt down to open the padlock, but his hands were shaking so severely that he dropped the keys.

"Get out of the way—I'll do it," said the robber as he forcibly pushed Harry into the closet door frame. That was the last straw for the strained shelf. The sound of snapping wood was immediately followed by the thunderous roar of an avalanche of a couple hundred pounds of Harry's prized collections. Harry stood motionlessly for a moment before realizing what had happened.

When he looked down, he saw the robber's lower legs jutting out from the mountain of boxes. The man was not moving, not making a sound. Harry rushed to the telephone and dialed 911. After he explained that an armed robber was in his house, the dispatcher assured him that the police were on their way. In his typically meek voice, Harry told the dispatcher, "I believe that the gentleman may need an ambulance."

No one was more shocked than Harry to see himself touted as a hero in the next day's newspaper. "Burglar Seeks Cash—Gets Concussion," read the headline.

"Oh, honey, I'm so proud of you!" Joan gushed as she hugged her husband. But Harry's thoughts were elsewhere. With the hefty reward, he could now buy a collector's cabinet. And that meant room for more cards and books!

SAMUEL D. BESKET

STRANGE ENCOUNTER
Angels are Walking Among Us

Sitting in his car in the driveway, Darrin could barely remember the drive home. "I can't believe this is happening!" If things weren't bad enough with his wife Jean drowning in Wills Creek last summer; now he was fired from his job. How long will these nightmares last? he pondered. How am I going to pay all my bills? Laying his head on the steering wheel, Darrin sighed, "I need to rest so I can sort this out tomorrow."

Early the next morning he laid all the bills on the dining room table. It didn't take long to see that he owed the local doctor the most. Picking up the phone he made an appointment for later that day to discuss his options. May as well get this over with, he thought. No way will I be able to pay all these bills now with no job or insurance. Driving into the parking lot, Darrin noticed it was empty except for a red Corvette with a flat tire, parked in the corner. This is about as close as I'll ever get to one of those, he thought as he walked in.

The atmosphere in the office was as cold and pristine as a winter night. The walls and furniture all blended together and were void of color. Sitting behind glass windows, in a white starched uniform, was a stone-faced receptionist. The only sign of life was a man about 20 years younger than him leafing through a magazine.

"Anything interesting in there?" Darrin asked as he sat next to him.

"It's *Newsweek* and it's four months old," the man replied.

" Sure can think of a better way to spend the afternoon; I said, it's nice outside."

"I know, my country club is having a golf outing this afternoon, but first things first."

Country club...., I bet that Vette sitting outside is his, probably here to play golf with the doctor after I leave, Darrin thought.

Sitting next to the stranger reminded Darrin how different their lives were. Raised by a single mom in poor health, he had struggled with finances all his life. I bet he never mowed lawns or delivered papers when he was growing up, he thought.

Shaking his head Darrin tried to think positive. "When God closes one door he opens another," Father Sam had told him. Suddenly, Darrin realized the stranger was touching his shoulder. "Are you alright? he asked, you were mumbling."

"Considering the circumstances, I'm about as good as I ever will be. I lost my wife, my job and medical benefits recently. I owe the doctor over $5,000 and don't know how I will pay him. Sorry, I shouldn't burden you with my problems."

Sliding over next to Darrin, he responded by telling him how we all have different burdens to bear. "You're right. Is that your Vette in the parking lot?" Darrin said, trying to change the subject.

"It gets me around,' he replied. "I have next year's model on order."

I bet he doesn't know his right rear tire is flat, Darrin thought. He'll find out soon enough. The next 20 minutes passed in a daze. Darrin knew the man was talking to him, but he was too depressed to listen. It seemed like he was in a tunnel filled with echoing voices. Father Sam said to pray and be positive, but Darrin had a difficult time doing that sitting here next to "Joe Cool."

"Can I get you something to drink; they have coffee over by the magazine rack," the stranger said.

"Coffee would be fine," Darrin replied.

Setting the cup down, the man told Darrin to keep his spirits up. "Things are always darkest right before dawn," he commented.

Turning, the stranger walked to the receptionist desk. "Wow, look at the big smile he gets. I bet they won't smile when I tell them I can't pay my bill," Darrin mumbled.

Walking toward the door, the stranger paused and turned to Darrin.

STRANGE ENCOUNTER **5**

"Remember the words of your priest." With that he left the building.

Better get this over with, Darrin thought tapping on the receptionist's window. "I would like to see what we can do to help pay my bill. I lost my job, and with my wife dying last year, I'm pretty well tapped out," he said.

Scrolling through her computer files she asked for Darrin's last four digits of his social security number. After several minutes the girl looked up. "I can't find any bill for you. Are you sure you have the right doctor's office? As a matter of fact, we have no outstanding bills for you at all." "What!!, Darrin shouted." How can that be? There has to be a mistake."

"Sir," the girl replied, "we don't have a bill for you. It must have been a computer glitch that sent you a bill in error."

Looking toward the door, Darrin paused, then returned his gaze to the girl. "Did the man driving the Vette pay my bill? Tell me it isn't so."

Looking a little bewildered the girl asked, "What man are you talking about?"

"The one I've been talking to for the last 30 minutes,"

"I don't know what you're talking about, the girl replied. You are the only appointment we had this afternoon."

Frustrated, Darrin shouted, "You're telling me I've been sitting here the last 30 minutes by myself? You didn't see another man in here talking to me?"

"Sir, please calm down, let me explain. The doctor doesn't see patients in the afternoon. We are here because you called and asked to talk to us about your bill, you just walked into the office. We don't know what bill you are talking about. Sir, are you OK? Maybe you'd better sit down."

Darrin's mind was spinning. It seemed he was asleep and couldn't wake up. Vaguely he heard the girl call 911 for a unit to respond for a confused patient before he drifted off to sleep.

He awoke to the realization of being in a hospital room. "Welcome back," Father Sam said smiling. "We need to talk and I have a book for you to read."

Laying a book on his bed, Father Sam stood up. "If you get dressed,

I'll drive you home."

Darrin read the title: "Angels Walking Among Us." Opening the book Darrin was startled by a picture of an angel driving a red Corvette.

JOY L. WILBERT ERSKINE

THE SPITTING CHAMPION
It Really Is the Little Things That Count

It wasn't your usual lofty life goal, but Martina had looked forward to this day since she was seven, when her 10-year-old brother, David, taught her the basic principles back home in Senecaville, Ohio. For the past five years, she had planned and prepared. Martina wanted to spit into the Grand Canyon.

David was a good spitter. He could launch a watery wad of wet 12 feet at that age and hit a target dead center from nine. "It's all in the lips," he explained. "You have to get a real good pucker going or you might as well be drooling."

Under David's tutelage, Martina got pretty good at it. They spent hours in the yard perfecting techniques. She tried hard, but never attained David's elevated stature in the field of expectoration.

The year Martina started junior high, David pitched for a Senecaville farm baseball team. His favorite was, naturally, the spitball but he saved that specialty for games when his team was falling behind.

One Saturday afternoon in the spring of 1923, David rocketed a nice juicy spitball toward home plate. He anticipated a satisfyingly liquid splat. There was a splat all right. The bat cracked and the returning baseball connected squarely with David's face. Blood, teeth, and saliva splattered everywhere. "Time out!" he screamed. Martina dashed to his side and watched, horror-stricken, as his face swelled to the size of a cantaloupe.

From that moment on for the rest of his life, David could not spit. Martina, who idolized him, was devastated. She vowed, "David, if

8   THE WILLS CREEK CHRONICLES

you can't spit, then neither will I."

Over the years, Martina had held to that promise. David was gone now, but Martina's adoration for her brother lived on. At age 89, Martina stood primly at the rim of the Grand Canyon, looking down on the Colorado River far below.

With the ease of long ago, Martina let fly a wondrous milky-white missile. It sailed 18 feet out over the canyon like a startled pigeon, then rocketed straight down. Minutes later, echoing back, a distinct "SPLAT!" was heard by the assembled crowd of onlookers. "Ooh!" was their enraptured response.

Martina grinned rakishly, blushing at their approval, then looked to the skies. "That, David, was for you," she whispered.

BARBARA KERNODLE-ALLEN

Granny's Revenge
Sweet Appearing Granny Gets Even With Wrong-doers

Trembling, A.J. cowered beneath the lilac bush in the squishy mud. A twig poked his bare belly. Afraid to move, he left it there, trying to comprehend what had happened. Believing himself to be an important man, good-looking for his age, a building contractor by trade, a township trustee, a church elder, he planned to run for county commissioner next year.

His wife would be worried, wondering why he is late. A mosquito buzzed past his face. Automatically, his long tongue flicked out and snatched it…"Slurp…Gulp."

A.J.'s mind screamed, "OH, GOD, NO"…"This is a nightmare… I'll wake up soon." Trying to will himself awake, he wiggled deeper into the mire.

A.J. saw two cats closing in on him. Feeling small and helpless, he trembled as the orange tabby blinked her golden eyes, licked her lips, stretched and yawned. The black and white cat with a black patch over one eye sat staring, licking his paw and other more private parts.

A skunk emerged from a nearby hollow log. Sniffing about for grubs, scratching in the dirt for dinner, he said, "Welcome to the group."

Panting, a small spotted dog raced about. "What did you do? Huh? Huh? What was it? Huh? Why was she mad at you? Huh? Huh?"

"What's going on? " A.J. croaked. "How can you animals be talking? Why do I understand you?"

The orange tabby waved her fluffy tail. Haughtily she explained….

"That sweet old lady in the house by the creek seems nice. The neighbor children like her, call her Granny. She bakes cookies, sings in the church choir, volunteers at the hospital. But cross her and you will see she is a real witch."

"What did you do? Huh? Huh?" the little dog coaxed.

The cat with the black patch over one eye spoke next. "I was a used car salesman.

Made salesman of the month three months in a row. Sold Granny a Dodge Aspen with a slant six engine. A great car, but the rust had been painted over. She was furious when the rust bloomed. She wanted her money back. When I said I couldn't, she called me a black- hearted pirate. I've been like this since 1985." Sadly he said, "She laughs when I lick my butt."

Shaking his head regretfully, skunk sighed. "All I did was light my cigar. When she asked me to put it out, I refused. That was three years ago. I sure miss those cigars."

The orange tabby cleared her throat. "I was a school teacher," she stated proudly.

"I spanked her grandson. Now she spanks me when I scratch my claws on her furniture."

Little dog whined, "I couldn't help it. I was late for work. I didn't have time to find a rest room, so I peed in her shrubbery by the road. They found my car in Wills Creek by Eighth Street road last winter... soooooo...what did you do, toad? Huh? What...?"

Beginning to understand, A.J. drew in a sobbing breath. "Granny hired me to build a room on the back of her house. She was clear about what she wanted, but I needed to cut corners to save some money. I thought she'd be easy to fool. I didn't brace the floor properly, installed cheap fixtures, and didn't put felt under the shingles. When the dry wall cracked, the door wouldn't close and the roof leaked, she called me. I told her it was too late. I couldn't do anything for her."

Suddenly, Granny appeared in the doorway, her white, fluffy hair surrounding her angelic face like a halo. The scent of warm cookies wafted through the opening. Wiping her wrinkled hands on her gingham apron, she set her rosebud mouth in a thin line. Lips pursed, she accused, "You've been talking to each other again. I am not pleased." With a curt nod, she closed the door.

Thunder rumbled. A bolt of lightening struck a tree on the ridge. Cold sheets of rain pelted the miserable little group. The skunk scrambled back into his log. The cats and dog took cover under the porch, and A.J. sat shivering in his puddle of slime, muttering, "How could she do this to me? "

Reappearing, the old lady glared at the toad. "I did not turn you into a toad. You were always a toad …a big toad in a little puddle. I merely removed your disguise."

Crouching under the lilac, rain running down his back, trying to resist the worm wriggling at his feet, A.J. sighed.

"Slurp…Gulp…YEECH!"

RICHARD A. DAIR

JIMMY-JOE'S FIRST LOVE
Everyone In Town Admired Her

*J*immy-Joe was a young man in his teens. He lived near Cambridge Ohio, in the 1880's. He worked hard every day and for the times had amassed a good savings. Then one day he saw something he just had to have, even if it took all that he had.

It was the first of the month, and like clock work, Jimmy-Joe was at the door of the First National Bank of Cambridge waiting for it to open. He and his family lived on a small farm along Wills Creek. When he wasn't helping his pa he would often do odd jobs for neighbors. His ma instilled in him the importance of saving his money.

"Never know when something special might present itself," she'd say." If you're broke, you might miss out. He didn't know then how special that little nugget of wisdom would become.

"Hey, Jimmy-Joe," came the cheerful greeting as the big oak doors of the bank swung open.

"Hey back too ya, Mr. Beckman," Jimmy-Joe said as he made his way to the deposit window. Alice Crabtree was already waiting behind the deposit window. She was a nice enough lady, her hair was tightly bound in a bun, fashionable for the day. In her 40's she was portly and overly friendly. Alice was desperate to marry off her daughter and mentioned her every time he came in. "Good morning Jimmy-Joe, what can I do for you this morning?" she chirped.

"Oh, just the usual. I managed to save pert near five dollars this month."

"My that going to put your balance over $200. You keep this up and you will be the richest man in Guernsey County. By the way have you met my daughter Beatrix?"

Jimmy-Joe politely said no and hurried out the door. He had met her alright. Nice enough girl but she was dog ugly. Outside he peered at his bankbook. Someday he'd have a need for all that money, but for now it just felt good knowing it was there.

That's when he noticed her. His eyes zeroed in on her as she walked down the street. Her long flowing mane of auburn hair rippled and gleamed in the morning sun. Her shapely legs long and strait. She carried herself like royalty. Mesmerized, Jimmy-Joe knew it was love at first sight.

'Pretty little thing," came a voice from behind him. "I've had my eye on her myself.

Startled Jim-Joe wheeled around. It was old man Jenkins.

"What do you mean, I wasn't looking. Just peering down the street is all."

"Now son, no need to be embarrassed, shucks, ain't a man in the tri-county area that hasn't envisioned himself partnered up with her. Yes sir, she's right fine."

"More than fine, she's perfect. Don't suppose I could get a closer look, do ya?"

"I wouldn't try it, Jenkins cautioned. That feller she's with is a might protective, they say he's extremely jealous and has roughed up more than one hombre that got too close."

"I don't care, it would be worth an ass kickin' just to get a closer look."

"Boy I think you've gone plum loco on me."

"Don't care, I've made up my mind. I just have to take the chance. Hopefully he will understand. Besides he should be proud that others admire her."

"Damn son, Yer either the bravest man I ever knew, or the dumbest. I'll stay back here, you might be needin a doc. If it starts to go bad fer ya, I'll go fetch him."

Too late, Jim was already half way down the street before Jenkins finished his sentence.

14   THE WILLS CREEK CHRONICLES

"Excuse me sir, He said. Your companion is very beautiful."

"Yep, she sure is, what's it to you?" came the gruff reply.

"Nothing really, I just wanted to compliment you on your fine taste, that's all."

"You're right , I do. Shame I have to leave her behind. I'm heading back east on the afternoon train, and I don't figure on coming back this way. I've had my time with her, but there's better back home. Thought I'd find someone to take her off my hands, but everyone seems afraid to talk to me, except you. You wouldn't be interested, would you?" Jim-Joe could hardly believe his ears or his luck.

"Oh yes sir, I surely would."

"Now not so fast, she comes with a lot of baggage I've bought her. I'd be losing out if I couldn't recoup some of it. I figure $200.00 would cover it. Ya got $200, young fella?' the man asked.

Beaming with joy, Jim-Joe assured him he had. He would go to the bank and be back shortly.

Alice Crabtree almost fainted as she handed Jimmy-Joe the $200, dashing all hopes for her Beatrix. But he didn't wait to explain.

"Here's your money,"he said.

"Well I'll be, you did have the money."

"I've been saving it for something special.

"She's special alright, and now she's all yours." That said, the man turned and headed for the train station.

That afternoon, beaming with pride for all to see Jimmy-Joe rode down the center of town on his new horse. All eyes were on them. Everyone said they made the perfect couple.

DICK METHENEY

WHO KILLED SHERYL?
Was It For Love Or Money?

Even in the pitch dark, Robert Dillon walked along the side of Route 821 closest to the trees. He kept in the shadows as much as possible, just in case he heard a vehicle approaching. If his lucky streak continued tonight, he just might get away with murder.

He knew sooner or later someone would find his wife's body in Wills Creek. If anyone remembered seeing him in this area, the best he could hope for would be life in prison. Walking along the deserted blacktopped road, he went over the act in his mind.

The first three years of their married life had been great. Sheryl seemed happy and content. But gradually the marriage went sour, happiness changed to boredom and then to quarrels and loud arguments. On their third anniversary after too much to drink, she calmly admitted to having an affair with a friend's husband. She showed no signs of remorse or regret.

After several weeks of bitter arguments, she begged for forgiveness and swore it would never happen again. That promise lasted almost a year and in the midst of a minor quarrel she had thrown the details of her newest affair into Robert's face. He began to think of ways to get out. It was a complicated situation. His wife and her brother, Joe Grismer, owned a small manufacturing company. While Robert was a minority stockholder, he did in effect work for the two of them. His contract left him no way to leave the company without losing his investment.

In desperation, he went to an out-of-town lawyer for advice. When

16 THE WILLS CREEK CHRONICLES

he had explained the situation he asked, "Is there any way for me to get out of this agreement?"

"Not in any court in this state."

After visiting the lawyer, Robert spent a long time thinking of possible ways to extricate himself from this intolerable situation. It was apparent that Sheryl had to die. Eventually, he came up with a plan, then spent another year revising it, until he was satisfied with the scheme.

For the next two years Robert hoarded every dime he could get his hands on without Sheryl finding out. He used the money to buy a new identity. While they lived in the same house, they did not live as man and wife during that time.

He'd worked diligently to remove as much of the risk as possible from the plan. If things went wrong, there was a set of documents hidden that gave him a new identity, complete with a car registered to that name. All he would have to do was get in the car and drive away.

When everything was in place, he waited patiently for the right situation. Suddenly the opportunity was staring him in the face. Joe sent him to Columbus in the evening in order to be there bright and early the next morning to meet with a new client. This was a common enough occurrence. Usually it meant Sheryl had a new lover and she wanted Robert out of the way.

Robert left work early, pleading a slight case of stomach flu. He went straight home to dose Sheryl's favorite bottle of wine with chloral hydrate, enough to ensure she would be asleep for several hours. He carefully wiped his prints off the bottle and liquor cabinet.

As usual, when Sheryl arrived home from work she poured herself a glass of wine. In less than 30 minutes she was out like a light. He carefully carried her to the garage and put her in the passenger seat of her Mini Cooper, clicking the seat belt around her. Returning to the house, he dumped the remaining wine down the sink and rinsed out the bottle, before tossing it in the trash. He washed her glass, carefully dried it and replaced it in the cabinet.

Scarcely half an hour later, he had Sheryl buckled in the driver's seat of her Mini, the car pointing downhill toward a sheer drop of about 40 feet into 16 feet of water. She had been showing signs of waking up for the last few minutes. It was the moment of truth; he could stop now with little or no damage done. The alternative was to stay married to Sheryl, and that he could not do.

Sheryl made his decision for him. Sleepily she muttered, "Mike, where are you? I can't get enough of your loving." Reaching in the open window Robert placed his gloved hand on the back of her head and slammed her forehead forward into the steering wheel with all his might. He quickly pulled the shift lever into drive and released the parking brake.

The car lurched forward down the incline to the edge of the drop. It stopped on the edge perfectly balanced for a long second, then plunged over into the cold dark water. Robert stood on the creek bank for ten minutes and watched the last bubble float to the surface. He was free at last!

In Columbus the next morning, Robert gave his sales presentation. After a brief conference the company reps accepted his offer. He called Joe and gave him the good news, then called home to leave a message for Sheryl. After a fast food lunch, he drove straight back to the office and, learning Joe had left work early, left the contracts on Joe's desk.

When Robert arrived home the first thing he did was check the message machine. He found his voice there along with two other male voices that did not identify themselves. They were calling for Sheryl and were not about to leave their names.

He called Joe at home. "Joe, do you have any idea where Sheryl is? It doesn't look like she's been here since yesterday."

Joe said, "Sheryl didn't come in to work today. I assumed she was working at home."

"There's a bunch of messages on the answering machine."

Joe said, "I'll call around and see if I could locate her."

In 20 minutes Joe called back, "Robert, have you heard from her?"

Robert let a little panic creep into his voice. "Joe, I think we should call the police. It looks like she has been missing since last night."

Joe tried to placate him, "Now, you just hold on. Sheryl is a big girl and she can take care of herself. Let's not do anything that will embarrass her. She might be visiting a friend or shopping or something. Let's wait for a little longer."

Robert knew Joe was just stalling to give Sheryl time to ditch the new boyfriend and come home. Joe knocked on his door just before

18 THE WILLS CREEK CHRONICLES

ten and walked in before Robert could reach the door. Right away Robert could see Joe was coming apart. The 40 dollar hair cut was messed up, the starched shirt was wrinkled and he was nervously puffing on a cigarette.

Joe asked, "Did you hear anything yet?"

Robert said, "Not a word. I think we better call the police. Sheryl's never stayed gone this long before."

"I know, I know. I keep hoping she'll walk through the door any minute. Let's give it another hour. If she doesn't show by eleven we'll call the cops."

"I'm going to make some coffee, you interested?" Robert asked.

"No, I could stand a good stiff drink. I'm cranked enough without any caffeine."

"Help yourself. I'm still going to make some coffee. I have a feeling it's going to be a long night." Robert wasn't about to drink anything alcoholic. He made the coffee with double the regular amount of grounds. It was strong and bitter. He drank it black to get the maximum effect from the caffeine.

When the clock on the mantle struck eleven, Robert picked up the phone and dialed 911. After the operator answered, Joe said, "My name is Robert Dillon and I want to report my wife missing."

Hours later, after telling his story over and over to Detective Manny Wilson, Robert was exhausted. He had continually sipped the strong coffee, but the caffeine was losing to the lack of sleep. He was barely coherent but still in much better shape than Joe. Those stiff drinks had hit him hard. After repeating his story to the detectives for the third time Joe just slumped over on the couch and started snoring. The detective looked at Joe with disgust plain on his face. "Does he always drink like this?"

"Not usually. He's worried about his sister. They were pretty close."

"Yeah, but she's your wife and I notice you ain't passed out drunk. How come?"

"I'm not much of a drinker. It doesn't do anything for me."

Out of the clear blue the detective asked, "Mr. Dillon, where did you dump her body?"

"What… what are you talking about?"

Detective Wilson said in a sympathetic voice, "I understand how this could happen. They screwed you out of your share of the company and your wife's chasing around with other men. You are about to lose everything you have worked so hard to achieve. I thoroughly understand how a thing like that could get to a guy. I found the wine bottle in the trash can. The fact that someone rinsed it out and wiped off any prints told me the whole story."

"No, you have it all wrong, detective. Think about it. If my prints were on the wine bottle it's no big deal, it's my home. I called several times to talk to her and left messages. Two of her lovers called looking for her. The only other person in Sheryl's life who didn't call was her brother Joe. It wasn't me and her lovers were obviously wondering where she was. The only other person in her life with anything to gain is her brother."

"Mr. Dillon, do you have any proof or are you just blowing smoke to cover your tracks?"

"Of course I don't have any proof. But if, as we both suspect, Sheryl is dead, I'll have to borrow the money to pay for her funeral. I know for a fact that the company has a cash flow problem. Joe needed her shares of stock to put up as collateral for a loan. I think he deliberately sent me to Columbus so he could kill her and blame it on me."

"Won't you inherit her estate?"

"I can't inherit if I'm found guilty of murdering her. Her life insurance goes to the company. If the company goes under, I lose the most. Her stock in the company will be worthless. This house and even the car I drive belong to the company."

Sheryl Dillon's body was found by fishermen nearly two weeks after Robert Dillon had reported her missing. Just before the end of his four-to-twelve shift that evening, Cambridge Police Detective Manny Wilson sat down at his desk to finish filling out the paperwork after the arrest of Sheryl Dillon's murderer..

Who did he arrest for the murder, her husband or her brother?

DONA McCONNELL

❦

ALL A MULE CAN DO

Home-Grown Wisdom to Stop a Disaster

"Let's git married."

"Are you crazy, Leroy?" Darlene said. "You have no money and no place to live." They were walking up the dirt road to Darlene's Pap's farm. The proposal came out of the blue and she was stunned.

Leroy puffed out his chest, preening proudly like a peacock at mating time. "I draw," Leroy said. "I git welfare and disability."

"But there's nothing wrong with you," Darlene rejoined.

"Sure thair is. My back hurts when I do stuff."

"My back hurts, too, when I work with Pap on the farm all day," Darlene said.

They rounded they corner to Pap's place. As usual, he was plowing the old-fashioned way, using his own father's hand plow, which was treated with more care than any family heirloom, and Old Bets, his faithful mule. For as long as Darlene could remember, every mule had been named Old Bets. At 91, Pap still walked straight and tall behind the heavy wooden plow with its sharp metal blade, struggling mightily to keep it in the row.

Pap paused when he saw Darlene. "Howdy, baby," he said. Darlene was his only granddaughter and clearly special.

"Pap, when are you going to get a John Deere and let Old Bets rest?"

"Aw, that old girl's doin' fine," he said. "It's me that's wearin out."

"Then get a John Deere so you can rest. You're not as young as you used to be."

ALL A MULE CAN DO **21**

"Oh, baby," Pap feigned heartbreak. "I'm just a spring chicken. "What you doin' here, Leroy?" he asked. He'd suspicioned Leroy was after Darlene and he didn't approve one bit.

"Just stopped by, Pap," Leroy said vaguely, absently digging his heel in the dirt.

Pap frowned. "Where's your geetar?"

The only time Leroy came by Pap's was to get his guitar tuned. Leroy played in a band with his three brothers, three strapping young men, all of who drew disability and claimed various ailments that precluded any form of labor. They could play guitar reasonably well, but none of them could tune one. Each time a gig was coming up, Pap was called upon to tune the guitars. If a string broke during play, the afflicted brother just sat down and the others finished.

They called themselves The Barrelheads, based on the time brother Ray Don stuck his head in a barrel of apples and couldn't get it out. The brothers thought it was a cool name, but most people agreed it was appropriate in an altogether different way. Especially Pap. Barrelheads, indeed.

"Darlene, honey, could you go inside and get me a cold drink. I'm about to fry out here."

The ruse worked and Darlene left Leroy and Pap alone.Pap got to the point quickly. "So, Leroy, what you doing with my Darlene?"

Leroy's head bowed low, avoiding Pap's piercing eyes. "I'm lookin' to marry her."

"You're a crazy fool," Pap said. "Darlene's got bigger plans than marryin' the likes of you."

"Well, all a mule can do is cry," Leroy said defensively. It was a phrase he and his brothers used, and no one knew if their speech was deficient in some way or if they simply didn't know any better.

"I can't keep you from tryin'" said Pap. "But Darlene's a smart girl. I've a mind to see her get married to a big-time banker or lawyer who'll build her a house on Wills Creek. Up there in that subdivision where you can see the creek from your back porch."

"Ain't nothin' wrong with Lone Holler that I can see," said Leroy.

That's exactly the problem, Pap thought, but instead he said, "You ain't even got a car."

"I can carry Darlene wherever she wants to go," said Leroy. "I'm strong and I carry my maw out to town on my back whenever she wants to go. Thirteen miles," he bragged.

"Lord a mercy," Pap said.

Darlene returned with lemonade for Pap and Leroy. "What you all been talking about?" she asked.

"Just shootin' the breeze," said Pap. He drank the lemonade and set the glass on the ground. "Better get back to my plowin,'Pap said and turned back to Old Bessie. "Darlene, why don't you stop by tonight and make an old man some of your special blackberry cobbler?"

"Sure, Pap," she said, waving as she and Leroy headed back down the dirt road.

"Dang loser," Pap muttered as he snapped the reins. Old Bets began her slow walk down the row. He'd nip this thing in the bud and he'd do it quick. Darlene had a good education and barrels of potential. Wasn' no way Leroy Potts would bring her down.

All afternoon Pap plowed and thought, thought and plowed. His mind sifted through a hundred possibilities. He'd only get one chance so his plan had to be a good one.

It was five o'clock when Darlene arrived with dinner. She'd brought pork chops and potatoes and the ingredients for the blackberry cobbler.

As usual, Pap enjoyed both her food and her company. Over coffee, Pap suddenly brightened. "Darlene, I've been thinkin' about this weddin' of yours and Leroy's. I've got some great ideas."

"What?" Darlene asked. "I thought you hated Leroy. You actually want me to marry him?"

"Well, honey, you know I'm a selfish old man. If you want Leroy, then Leroy it is."

Darlene was speechless, finally muttering, "Well, I hadn't totally decided..." Her voice trailed off.

"He's a might slow, but a good boy. Now I was thinkin' this. 'Cause Leroy ain't got much money, we'll have the weddin' right here at the farm. That spot up by the big oak would be perfect."

"But Pap, there's a herd of cows out there, some bulls, too."

"Nonsense, them cows won't pay you no mind. There's a lot of briers, and a bit of cow manure, I must say, but if you wear jeans you'll be fine."

"Jeans!" Darlene wailed, "For my wedding?"

"Well, honey, you can wear a white shirt or somethin'. Now you can't be askin' Leroy to pay for things he can't afford. That's no way to start a marriage." Before she could respond, Pap plowed on. "Then, after the wedding, Leroy can carry you down to his mama's for your honeymoon. It'll work out perfect."

"Carry me?" Darlene nearly yelled. "Why, it must be seven or eight miles. Besides, I don't want to spend my honeymoon with Leroy's mother." Her face registered stunned disbelief.

"Now there you go agin' askin for the moon. You know Leroy ain't got a car and he carries his mama all the way to town once a week. And there's no place else to live. I know Leroy's mama's got a bad reputation for meanness, but maybe she just needs somebody to take care of her, you know, do all the cookin' and cleanin' and stuff. That'd probably improve her mood one hundred percent.

"You'll have to drop out of school, of course," Pap continued. "But nobody here gets much education anyway. And there's Leroy's disability check."

Darlene started at her beloved Pap, speechless. How could he actually suggest such a thing? He'd always said she deserved a better life than what was available here in Lone Hollow.

"I reckon you'll be havin' babies real soon and you won't hardly notice Leroy's mom. It'll be just like havin' two babies. Real good practice…."

"Stop, Pap," Darlene said. "I don't want to get married. Especially to Leroy. I want things to stay just the way they are. I don't want to drop out of school. I want to be something, just like you're always telling me. I can be something, Pap. I don't want to live with Leroy and his mama and spend my whole life struggling and doing without. You said I could make a better life. Don't you still believe that?" Her voice was shaking and Pap could see tears forming at the edges of her eyes.

"Well, of course, honey," Pap said. "I was just tryin' to do what would make you happy. I thought maybe I was interferin' too much and just needed to let you have the man you wanted."

"I don't want Leroy!" she practically screamed. "In fact, I don't care if I never see him again."

24 THE WILLS CREEK CHRONICLES

"Well, it's whatever you want, honey bun," Pap said. "I guess I got it all wrong. Say, it's getting' late. You've got school tomorrow, so you'd better get goin'. Your mama says you've had tons of homework in the advanced class you got into. Says you ain't been getting' enough sleep."

"Yeah, I'd better get going, " she said as she composed herself. "Senior year is really hard, but my counselor says I've got a real shot at a scholarship to college."

"Why of course you do," Pap answered. "A brainy girl like you. Must git it after your Pap."

Darlene laughed. She loved Pap more than just about anybody. Even though he'd never had any schooling, he knew her better than anybody. Most important, he saw more in her than she'd ever seen in herself. "A young woman with a future," he called her and he'd made her believe it. "I guess so," she said as she hugged him goodbye.

The next day Leroy stopped by, his anger burning like a tire kiln.

"What'd you do to Darlene?" he demanded. "She won't hardly speak to me and just laughs when asked her about gittin' married. Says she won't be marrying anybody from this holler."

"Well, don't that beat all," Pap said. "I thought you two had it all settled when you came by yesterday."

"I know you did somethin'," Leroy said. "If you weren't an old half-foolish codger, I'd deck you right here. You stupid old fool, you've ruint my life."

With that, he spun on his heel and stalked away down the hill toward his mama's house.

Pap stood for a minute, wiping his brow with an old rag and letting Old Bets rest. "Well, he said softly to himself," all a mule can do is cry."

Then Pap laughed out loud, so hard and long that Old Bets threw back her head and let out a bray so enthusiastic that he gave her an apple from of his overall pocket. On a whim, he unhooked her from the plow, right in the middle of a row, and let her run free the rest of the day while he sat on the front porch, smoking his pipe and smiling a contented smile.

MARALYN COOPER O'CONNELL

A Bouquet of Limericks
Musings From Under An Old Oak Tree
On the Banks of Wills Creek

Of gardeners there's many a tale
With veggies and fruits by the pail
Just drop in the seeds
Keep after the weeds
And the dirt that grows under your nails.

With brothers and sisters today
What can you possibly say
Some may get along
Others get it all wrong
But let the chips fall where they may.

Two cats are more fun than one
When everyone has so much fun
They play and they romp
And occasionally stomp
When one is Atilla the Hun.

There once was a kitty named Brice
Who was naturally quite fond of mice
He brought them to dinner
"It's surely a winner"
"With gravy they'll be twice as nice."

A homemaker who tired of the drill
Such as cleaning each wall, floor, and sill
"I'll just go on strike"
"I'll do what I like"
Too much scrubbing and scouring can kill.

While pondering a roomful of clutter
Those living there were heard to mutter
"Let's clean up this mess"
"And end our distress"
"Then breakfast on pancakes and butter."

Vacation is really such fun
Relax and sit out in the sun
No deadlines to meet
Just put up your feet
And groan when vacation is done.

MARILYN DURR

THE BODY ON THE DOCK
A Dream Vacation, A Couple in Love, And a Body

Chuck and Jeanette Morgan finished breakfast and cleaned up. A bright sun cast light through the kitchen window inviting a leisurely stroll along the peaceful beach.

"This is the best vacation we've ever taken, I'm glad you surprised me." A smile beamed on Jeanette's face. In the past four years, they'd gone where Chuck wanted to go and those holidays always involved wild animals, snakes and mosquitoes deep in some Canadian wilderness where campers had to be flown in by plane. Feeling stranded and miserable, she spent the whole two weeks on the verge of hysterics. Wills Creek was wilderness enough for her.

"You never once complained when we went to north country and I know you hated it. I figured it was time to treat you to a vacation you'd enjoy. After all, this is our fifth anniversary," Chuck said.

She allowed him to pull her into his arms and kiss her soft, full lips.

"Let's go for our walk, we can play kissy-face later, you gorgeous male," she giggled, squirming out of his embrace.

They were greeted with a cool ocean breeze and the crisp smell of salty air. "Beat you to the dock," Jeanette yelled after she jumped from the steps onto the soft, warm sand.

An isolated beach house and deserted stretch of sand dunes on the ocean's edge was the best get-a-way her husband ever planned. She wished they hadn't forgotten their camera. *I could have sworn I packed it in my suitcase. Maybe one of those disposable cameras will* do. Jeanette decided to buy one when she drove into the village.

But first things first. She was on a beach with the man she loved on their fifth wedding anniversary. She wasn't about to waste time shopping when romance filled the air. "Hurry up slow-poke," Jeanette yelled when she reached the dock before Chuck.

Sitting on the edge of wooden planks with her feet dangling in the warm ocean, she noticed her husband's reflection in the gentle lapping waters. His expression terrified her. She screamed just before a rope tightened around her neck.

Her body lay on the dock in the hot sun for two weeks, sea gulls feasting on the corpse. Then a category four hurricane raged offshore three days before she was discovered.

Several weeks passed and finally, the beach house was rented for the first time that season. The leasing manager said the cottage sat empty all summer.

"Too many people stayed home this year because of the recession. That's why the place is so clean," she added.

An unidentified body on the dock wasn't mentioned. Neither were newspaper headlines or articles about a young, dead, blonde woman wearing a bikini and no jewelry being spotted by fishermen. Nothing was said by the leasing agent about the mystery surrounding this woman. No one knew she came from Cambridge, Ohio and lived along the banks of Wills Creek.

Investigators hadn't found any clues. Speculations surfaced she washed up on the dock during hurricane Roscoe when a twenty-foot tidal surge hit the beach, swiping all evidence into the ocean. Stranger happenings were common place along this stretch of land.

No one reported a woman her age missing. Her husband never claimed her body.

Jane Doe was chiseled on the headstone for her name and underneath someone wrote the caption: ***The Body On The Dock***

PAM RITCHEY

THE LETTER
What Happened to Constance?

Attending auctions is one of my life's greatest pleasures. Searching for bargains, I followed the procession ranging from fancy cars to old pick-up trucks down a long overgrown lane. The abandoned farm house sat high on a hill overlooking Wills Creek. Little did I know what intrigue would be aroused with a letter I found in the lining of an antique trunk I purchased that day. From all appearances, the trunk sat in the attic undisturbed for more than 80 years:

If you're reading this, I too must be lost forever. I've gone to bring Laura back from the clutches of a demon. I only wish she could have been dissuaded from leaving with him, but no, she was too headstrong. She wouldn't even listen to God Himself as He touched her heart during that last Sunday's sermon. Promises of romance and riches have led her astray.

I know it was imposing and not quite proper, but I posted a letter telling her I was coming for a visit claiming to need the refreshment of country air to cleanse my ailing lungs.

The evil of the place engulfed me upon alighting from the carriage. What was once a beautiful rose bush is now nothing but a stick with thorns. Other flowers, once well tended, have dried as though touched by a harsh arid wind. The vegetable garden sits wilted except for strange herbs I have no recollection of ever seeing.

Tonight is All Hallows Eve. I am filled with apprehension on what may occur to my misdirected baby sister. I followed her last night as they sneaked away thinking me sleeping from the mixture he has

30 THE WILLS CREEK CHRONICLES

been placing in my night-time tea. Managing to sop some up in my handkerchief, they thought most of it gone.

As they neared the edge of the forest, a path appeared with a wave of his arm! While they made their way into the mist, my dearest Laura was giggling from the spell he has cast over her. Though trembling with fear, I followed. They came out in an opening with a large stone slab in the middle, engraved with the oddest of symbols. It seemed as if they were preparing for an un-Godly ritual.

Running quickly ahead of them as they returned to the house, I managed to leap into my bed and under my coverlet before Laura came to check on me. Unusual though, she stayed for a moment and whispered the strangest chanting. I couldn't make out the words but must have been soothed by them as the next thing I remember is waking up to bright sunshine this morning.

Laura was quite the hostess today, humming happy tunes and granting my every wish. She even sat and listened as I pleaded with her to leave with me. I cannot believe she questioned my purity, though; Asking if my virginity had been snatched from me. But, she apologized, patted my hand and said everything would be over soon. I will go first thing in the morning to fetch a carriage to take us from this dreadful place.

I managed to sop up some of my drink again tonight. I wonder… Oh, wait, I hear footsteps approaching, many voices! Who's out there? Laura's softly calling "Constance, I've a surprise for you," and that strange chanting. Very tired…must hide this…

J. PAULETTE FORSHEY

Uncle Eugene
A Man And His 'Experience' One Dark And Lonely Night

You'll have to ignore Uncle Eugene when he starts a stare'n and mumble'n. Since his 'experience,' that's what we kin calls it , deep in those woods alin'n muddy ol' Wills Creek, Uncle Eugene just hasn't been right. Not saying he was before but well before we just thought he was a little slow. His problems got a whole lot worse after the 'experience.'

It started one dark and stormy night. Uncle Eugene and Fred, that be Uncle Eugene's Redbone Hound, were alone in the cabin. Everything was fine. Uncle Eugene had a cozy fire going, rabbit stew with fresh greens, and sweet baby onions in the pot. The roof and the wall chinking were tight and dry. Alice Kirby been by earlier and left a criss-cross apple pie. Before Uncle Eugene's 'experience', she was sweet on him. Uncle Eugene and Fred were cozied up like a hog in deep mud.

Uncle Eugene headed from the table with his plate to fill it when the lantern and the fire went out. Plum strange because Uncle Eugene yousta make a good fire. A log snapped and popped in the hearth. That's when old Fred growled low and deep in his throat kinda like when a Red Bone corners something a lot bigger than hisself. That's when everything else gets real quiet and the hair sticks up on the back of your neck and arms. Well there stood Uncle Eugene not sure to go forward or back and Fred growling and moving around the room.

Uncle Eugene couldn't hear anything but the wind and rain and old Fred growling. Then the cabin door busted open and something come tumbling in.

Well, let me tell you, Uncle Eugene was pretty scared about then. Fred must have latched on to the thing and it must have latched on to Fred. There was all kinds of growling, howling, and chomp'n.
Uncle Eugene wasn't sure to go forward or back with all that going on. He said it was if the devil himself had latched on to a catamount's tail. The fighten' continued for a ways before old Fred and the thing went barreling out the busted cabin door. Then it got real quiet. Scary quiet.

Uncle Eugene stood there listening to the wind, rain, and the quiet in the cabin. Then the lantern and the fire flared back up. The cabin was all teared up, the cook pot was licked clear clean, and so was the pie tin.

Uncle Eugene looked at his tore up cabin 'til first light not sure if he should go forward or back. That's how we found him three days later. We bring him down to our place in Cambridge and offered him the spare bed, seeing he's kin and all, but come nightfall Uncle Eugene went and barricade hisself in our shed. Now, every morning, he comes out and sits on our front porch. Eats his meals there, rocking hisself in a chair that doesn't do that. Then come nightfall, off he goes to the shed. He don't trouble anyone most times. Uncle Eugene just been stuck like that in his head. Not sure if'n he should go forward or back. Until he decides, I guess he'll be living in our shed. That's ok, he's kin and all.

Well if you'll excuse me I better git some squezzins to help Uncle Eugene get by with his 'experience'. 'Til then you'll have to ignore Uncle Eugene.

LINDA BURRIS

Pa and Ma Go to Town
There's Interesting Talk About The New Preacher

It was a sunny, spring day on the Oswald farm. Ma and Pa were sitting in the screened-in back porch contemplating about taking a trip to town. The town, of 600 people was near Wills Creek between Cambridge and Byesville. It was a town where everyone knew most of their fellow citizens.

"Ma, sighed Pa, "you ready to go yet? We should be a goin' iffn' you want to do some visitin' fer a spell with the townfolk."

"Pa, I'm ready iffn' you are. I've got a whole bunch of folk I'm hankerin' to see in town."

They got in their old, battered Ford 1954 pickup truck. When started it started a 'shakin' and Ma made sure their seat belts were fastened. Pa put the truck in drive and off they went.

"Pa, I want to stop at the bank. I might want to buy something pretty for the house. Go through the drive-thru winder. Those tubes goin' back and forth jest are fascination' to me. I love that swoosh sound it makes and talkin' to the drive-thru lady. Here's the paper filled out for our money."

Pa put the tube in the drive-thru drawer, pushed the button and off the tube swooshed back to the drive-thru lady. In a couple of minutes the tube swooshed back and Pa removed the money envelope.

"Pa, where you want to go next?"

"Let's go see Harvey at the hardware store. I need a new saw. My old one has a cracked blade cause I used it on the pig when I was chasin' him tryin' to git him back in his pen, and some new fencin' and four-penny nails," he said.

"I'm goin' to the library and gettin' some more mystery books. I jest love reading those books of Mary Lu Warstler about those cats and her church folk. The lady preacher helps the sheriff solve who killed a stranger in her flower garden or the man behind the pipe organ. Mysteries and a book on astronomy, so I'll know what I'm seein' through my telescope at night. I hope to talk to Joy Erskine, some fine lady who really knows a lot about writin' too. See you in an hour outside the diner for lunch."

At the diner Marilyn Durr took their orders. They were eating light today. Pa ordered a sirloin steak with baked potato and green beans, the special. Ma, who hoped to keep her girlish figure a while longer, opted for a green salad and green tea with a splash of lemon.

Marilyn returned in a few minutes with their lunch. Ma said to her, "Have you seen the new preacher yet? I hear his wife is 10 years older than him?"

"All I can tell you right now is he's 6'5" and looks like a big, soft teddy bear with his big belly. The wife has gray hair at her temples and the color of her hair is probably out of a bleach bottle.'

Pa looked at Marilyn, "You don't say. How does he preach?"

"Well, replied Marilyn, "His hair is soooooooooo black and he has pimples on his dimpled cheeks and an earring in his left ear. I also heard that he has a tattoo on his chest, a red heart with an arrow going through it with his wife's name on it."

Ma looked so surprised of the description of the new preacher that her mouth opened wide enough to catch a fly.

Pa said, "How does he preach?"

"Well, he says there is a hell to shun and a heaven to gain. He pounds on the pulpit and his face turns red, he gets his hanky out and wipes his brow. Then he speaks about 20 minutes about Jesus comin' to take his children to Heaven. He sings like a sweet mourning dove and looks like Santa Claus when he laughs. Loves to give hugs to everybody and tells them that Jesus loves them and he does too."

"Ma we better git goin', the grocery store will be closing soon."
"Okay. I hope Rick carries out our groceries again. He's such a nice lookin' boy. He wants to be a newspaper reporter after he gets his journalism degree. He's always lookin' for a good story from his

customers. I hear he gets a lot of tip money that he's savin' for college.

At the grocery Ma and Pa got their weekly staples: Eggs, bacon, lard and doughnuts with white powdered sugar. They also got coffee, chocolate ice cream, potato chips, and cat food for their dog Sarge.

"We've had quite a trip to town today. I think when we get home that I'll take a nap before supper. Don't forget to feed Sarge his cat food and I"ll slop the pig after supper," said Pa.

"Pa, I could use a nap too. All that talkin' about the preacher an' all jest tuckered me out. On Sunday we better go to church to see for ourselves this new preacher and his wife."

DONNA WELLS

❦

THE WITCH OF WILLS CREEK
Hocus Pocus

No one knew exactly when she first appeared in the area. It seemed as if one day she just materialized and began living in the old rundown cabin near Wills Creek. She lived there alone except for her cat and dog. Occasionally the residents of Pleasant City would see her in town doing some shopping. She never spoke to anyone.

Even without makeup she was beautiful. Tall and slender, her hair, cascading to her shoulders, was midnight black. She had mesmerizing eyes.

Sheriff Tom Mayberry and his deputy, were discussing her over breakfast one morning at the diner on Main Street. Deputy Doug could not help thinking of her. "Boss, what do you think we should do about that strange lady out at the old Stoker cabin?"

"Not sure what we can do Doug, I can't think of any law that she has broken, except maybe trespassing, but I'm not sure it's worth the trouble. No one has ever complained, not even the owner of the property. Actually, I'm not even sure who owns that neck of the woods."

Doug frowned "Did you know that there is a rumor going around town that some folk, think she might be a witch."

"Yeah Doug, I've heard that, but I, for one, don't really know or care."

"The other night when you sent me out to patrol the highway about 13 miles south of town, I swear I heard howling."

The sheriff laughed, "Doug, don't let your imagination get the best

THE WITCH OF WILLS CREEK **37**

of you just because you happened to hear a dog howling on a night when there was a full moon."

"Well if you don't mind sheriff, I think I'll take a ride out there after breakfast."

"Do what you want. There is nothing much going around here anyway."

After breakfast, Doug drove his cruiser to the edge of the woods near the cabin. There was a large dead tree lying across the driveway that led up to the cabin. He got out of the car and found a note tacked on a nearby that tree that read "WARNING, this area is protected by the Blair Witch Project - enter at your own risk."

Doug felt goose bumps on his body and the hairs on the back of his neck stood up. He remembered the howling that he had heard the last time he was near here. Then he thought about how the sheriff had made fun of him. Ignoring his qualms, he climbed over the huge log as he walked toward the cabin.

When he stepped into the clearing, where the old cabin had sat for years and years, Doug was shocked. He had expected to see a run down shack. Instead there was a small cabin that looked like it had just appeared out of a fairy tale. It had the look of a gingerbread house, straight out of a Mother Goose book.

Everything seemed new, the roof, the logs, and the landscaping around the building looked professional. There was a strange aroma as he got close to the house. He also took notice of the cauldron sitting in the yard, next to a picnic table. There was a pentacle hanging from the gable over the front door. A broom was propped up next to the door. A black kitten sat in the sun grooming itself. A large, black Labrador dog was on the front porch guarding the cabin.

Carefully, Doug stepped around the dog and murmured, "Nice doggy, good boy."

The dog looked up and wagged its tail; Doug breathed a sign of relief, and rapped softly on the door. There was no answer. He was rapping harder when a voice behind him said,

"Can I help you?" Doug jumped about a foot and spun around. When did she appear, he thought.

"You need not worry about the dog, Satan won't hurt you."

Up close, he thought she was the most beautiful woman he had ever seen. Her hair was pulled back into a ponytail and she was wearing a black sweat suit, which accented her violet eyes.

Words stuck in Doug's throat. Finally he chocked out a, "Hello, my name is Doug; I just stopped by to say hello."

She answered, "That was very nice, thank you."

"Well then, I'll just be on my way, sorry if I bothered you."

"No problem, as long as you are here, may I offer you a cup of tea. By the way, my name is Stephanie, friends call me Stevie."

Doug began to sweat, now what do I do, he thought, if I drink her tea will I turn into a goat or a toad? His mind was racing, if I refuse, will she turn me into a toad anyway? As long as I am still in one piece, I had better go along with whatever she suggests. Plus I cannot seem to take my eyes off her.

She led the way into the cabin, and he followed. The house was spotless. There was a strong aroma of incense and candles everywhere, and herbs were hanging from the ceiling to dry. Despite his misgivings, Doug felt the interior of the house had a warm, cozy ambiance. She poured the tea. Doug hesitantly took a sip. The taste of the tea was somewhat familiar but Doug just couldn't place it. Along with the tea, she placed a large slice of cake in front of him. He thought, Devils food cake, of course, what else.

Doug was afraid not to drink the tea or eat the cake, just in case. As they sat there, Doug tried making small talk. His throat was dry and his muscles tense, "The cabin looks great. I haven't been here since I was a kid. I expected the place to be falling down"

"Oh no, I tore down the old place. Everything here is brand new."

"May I ask, how did you happen to pick this spot near Wills Creek?"

"The old cabin just happened to be on the forty acres that I inherited from my Aunt Druzilla."

"Oh I see, actually my boss was wondering if you were trespassing."

"Does everyone think that I am trespassing? Is that why they all cross the street when they see me coming?"

Doug was beginning to feel braver, "that and the fact that the whole town thinks you're a witch."

"I'M A WITCH?"

"Yea, and now that I'm here, I can understand why they think that way. I have to be honest, I'm kind of afraid to drink the tea."

Stevie rocked back and forth with laughter, and tears were streaming down her face.

"Honestly miss; I don't see what's so funny."

"I am not a witch, never have been!"

"Then could you please explain the warning sign, and the cauldron, not to mention all the candles, incense, herbs, and crystals and stuff like that?"

"When I first came here, after my aunt died, it was obvious that teenagers were using the cabin for parties, so I put that sign up and had my contractor chop down the tree across the driveway so that the kids couldn't drive up to the cabin."

"What about all the other stuff I mentioned. You have a black cat and a dog named Satan?"

"That was his name when I adopted him last year; he's a lot of company. I keep the cauldron and other things to put me in the mood so I can work."

"What do you do?"

"I'm an author, I write horror stories, Stephanie King, maybe you've heard of me. My last book was on the New York Times best seller list for 13 weeks."

DONNA J. LAKE SHAFER

J. P.'s Model "A" Ford
Changing From Horses To Cars Wasn't Easy

J.P. Hayes had a large farm bordering Wills Creek. There was a large house, a large barn, a large family and an equally large ego. He liked to show off his possessions and loved to be the first fella in the area to have any new gadget on the market.

J.P. had been mulling over the idea of car ownership. No one in the rural area where he lived had one. He wanted to be the first, seeing himself running into town on a Saturday afternoon with his wife and kids in a shiny new conveyance. Yessireee, that would really be a sight.

Old Man Hayes, as he was frequently called by non-family members, had looked into the matter and his heart was set on a Model "A" Ford two-seater. He'd seen one at the auto dealer store in town and it was probably still available. Hitching up the team, he called to Tommy, his oldest son, "Come on, boy, we're going to do us a little shopping."

Traveling the six miles along Wills Creek on a gravel road behind a team of draft horses took some time. But J.P. knew the trip back would be a thrilling experience.

In town, the team was hitched behind Smith Auto. J.P., followed by Tom, sauntered in, his bib overalls fairly bulging with bills. He loudly announced for anyone within shouting distance to hear, that he was there to buy a car.

Now, back in those days one didn't need a driver's license. All it took was the desire to own an automobile and money. J.P. had both.

He also had determination. So it wasn't long until Smith Auto had his cash and J.P. had a set of car keys. Soon, he was on his way home in his latest acquisition. Tom followed with the team.

Driving a car was a new experience for J.P., but he tooled along, gaining confidence and speed as he got closer to home. Sitting up straight, he never looked left or right as he passed the farms of his wide-eyed neighbors. Reaching his place, he entered the barn, never slowing, and crashed through the back wall smack into a wagon load of hay. The car shuddered, then stopped.

Brushing hay out of his hair and off his face, J.P. Hayes sputtered, "Dammit! When I say whoa, I mean whoa!"

That car remained in that spot for weeks, front-end wrinkled and covered with hay, before J.P. got up the nerve to drive again. Confidence shaken, he never got very good at it. The neighbors were glad that he left most of the driving to his boys, at least for a while, until they took to going up and down the road kicking up clouds of dust.

It wasn't long before everyone in the neighborhood had a car, but J.P. never let them forget that he had the first one.

LINDA WARRICK

LIFE IN THE CEMETERY
Through the Eyes of a Small Boy

As the sun sank below the horizon, a misty fog gathered slowly in the low areas of the Wills Creek Valley and the temperature dropped sharply. Though still light, the quarter moon was all ready visible in the graying sky on that crisp, cool night in early October of 1939.

Tommy pulled his tattered rag of a coat closer around his shoulders, wondering aloud where his uncle might be. Would he search for him or did he simply not care? For almost two weeks, Tommy had managed to survive the cold nights and slightly warmer days. He knew in his heart there had to be a better way; he just wasn't willing to take it.

Anything, even loneliness, was preferable to how he had been treated at the hands of his father's older brother.

If his dad had been the father he should have been, he would have never have had to live with his uncle in the first place. No one knew Dad's whereabouts and most didn't care.

Mom died when he was six of consumption. Uncle Brooks said Tommy was "lucky to have an uncle that was willing to take in the likes of him."

At first, Tommy thought Uncle Brooks would enjoy having him around, since he was the son he had never had. He would be someone that the older man could take hunting and fishing. But things didn't work out that way. Tommy was made to feel like a baby whenever he tried to hide his grief at the loss of his beloved mother. There were many more chores than there was free time. He had to work harder than any ten-year-old should have to.

It soon became clear that the flask was what Uncle Brooks lived for. He was mean and belligerent, often taking his frustrations out on Tommy. This wisp of a boy had been beaten, called profane names and deprived of food for no apparent reason. Tommy knew he had to get away. So one morning, instead of going to school, he gathered his few belongings into a burlap sack, along with the loaf of bread and some jerky he'd stolen from the kitchen, and headed out. He knew not where he would go, only that he could no longer stay with his uncle. He could not risk the abuse being repeated.

By the end of that day, he had walked several miles to the edge of the little town. He knew he had to find somewhere to stay before nightfall. As he rounded the bend in the worn, rutted road that ran along the banks of Wills Creek, he noticed, set back against the hillside and rimmed be a large grove of brush and trees, the old, abandoned graveyard.

Tommy had never paid much attention to cemeteries. They really didn't bother him; in fact, he was even a little bit comforted by them. After all, his mother was in one, where they told him she was "in a better place now".

Climbing the hill with his meager belongings, he scouted the area to find a niche that would afford some shelter. The lad knew his uncle would not likely find him here, if he even bothered to look. The terrain was hilly, but perhaps he could find a low spot to serve as a shelter where he could cover a ravine with some branches.

Tommy worked feverishly before the sun slipped behind the hill. Exhausted from pulling and carrying the brush, he laid down, using the burlap bag with his belongings to rest his head. After a few bites of his rations, he drifted off into a fitful sleep. But at least he was safe.

In the first fragment of a dream, he saw his uncle running after him and woke with his heart pounding wildly. Was it only a dream or was there a real threat? In his drunken stupor, his uncle would surely beat him badly. As the cobwebs cleared in his mind, the boy realized that he was safe in a cocoon of his own making.

Sometime in the middle of the night, he awoke again to the sound of a mournful howl in the distance. Not sure if it was one of the town's dogs or one of the wild variety, he shuttered from fear and the cold.

Toward morning, he awoke to the rustle of leaves. Remaining as still as possible, perhaps no one would guess he was there. Tommy soon realized that his fears were unfounded when he saw in the dim light, a large hare sniffing the air near him. It was comforting to know that he wasn't really alone in his little world.

As the morning sunlight crept over the hill, he rubbed his hands and shoulders to warm himself. If he was going to stay here, he was would have to find a way to keep warmer. Tommy then turned his attention toward the growling pain in his stomach. The remaining bread and jerky would not sustain him forever. Perhaps he should have re-thought his timing and waited to make his escape in the spring or summer when there would have been wild fruits and berries to help sustain him. But no, that was not an option, given the way things were when he left. No, he had done the right thing.

So how would he solve this problem of sustenance? There were not enough of a variety of plants to eat in the woods this time of year, but perhaps he could catch a fish if he could find a nearby stream, or find roots to dig. He recalled how he and some friends had previously had some success in catching squirrels.

Tommy had passed several days searching the cemetery grounds for things he could use. On one such excursion, he stumbled upon a weathered heap of wood from what was once the old caretaker's shed. He wondered if he could salvage enough to make it livable, or at least save enough wood from it to use for his shelter. Pieces of rusty metal, once used to anchor grave decorations could be twisted to hold branches together. He could use the sharper pieces to cut things. Fruit jars that had once held bouquets of flowers, though chipped, would hold rain water.

Tommy ventured into the deepening woods and followed a tiny trail, that had probably been trampled by deer. It led him to a babbling brook cascading down from some rocks. Now he would not have to depend on rain water and could even wash up a little.

After scrubbing his hands and face, he started back in the gathering dusk to return to his makeshift quarters. Tired, but determined, he added some more brush he had woven together for warmth and retreated beneath it.

Before he could get comfortable, he heard the distinct noise of a rumble on the hill above him. It couldn't be thunder; there wasn't a cloud in the sky and the sun was setting beautifully. Curiosity got the better of him. He crept slowly up the hill, crouching behind shrubs as he advanced.

Peering from the brush, Tommy saw a couple get out of a late model car and walk hand-in-hand, their eyes slowly scanning the headstones. Suddenly, they turned abruptly as they neared the edge of the hill. Tommy ducked, but too late. He had been spotted. Fear gripped him. What if he was made to return to his uncle?

The petite blonde lady was pretty. The gentlemen by her side was well-dressed and quite tall.

"What are you doing out here son?" the stranger asked.

"Uh," Tommy stammered, "Just lookin' for squirrels, sir."

"Don't you think it is getting kind of late for that? You know you are rather young to be this far from town by yourself,"the man replied.

"Uh, yes, sir, I will be going soon, sir." Tommy answered. What was he going to do or say now, if they persisted?

"What is your name young man?" the pretty lady inquired.

Tommy's heart was in his throat. Would he be in more trouble if he made up a name?

"Uh, it's Tommy, I mean Tom Camden."

The blood appeared to drain from the ladies' face, even in the low light of the growing dusk. "Oh, Steven!" she gasped. Steven barely caught her before she slumped to the ground.

As he held her, he said to Tommy, "Her name is Maureen and apparently she is your mother. She was told that you had died years ago and we came here in search of your grave."

"How could this be", a stunned Tommy thought, glancing down at the lady slumped in the man's arms. Could his father have not have wanted him and didn't want her to have him either?

As Maureen came to, she wondered, did she dare hope that this was "her" Tommy? Looking carefully at him, she noticed that the color of his hair and eyes did match her own, and she could see a resemblance of the boy she thought she had lost some four years ago.

Thus, Tommy's life in the cemetery came to an end. There was much catching up to be done. He could never have guessed that he would see his mother again. Someone had been watching out for him.

BEVERLY J. JUSTICE

ART FOR ART'S SAKE

An Extreme 'Neighborhood Watch'

Everything was unpacked finally, and Carol's apartment was beginning to reflect her eclectic tastes. Unmatched furniture and antique lamps surrounded a modern entertainment center. Her own paintings adorned the walls. Small pots of herbs occupied the kitchen window sills and a galloping horse on a beach towel separated the pantry from the kitchen.

Since the divorce Carol had been making ends meet by offering private art lessons and selling her work at art fairs. At the age of 32 she was eager to start a new life, one in which her dreams would no longer be dashed by an always disapproving husband. The duplex apartment with its spacious rooms offered Carol a haven to develop her artistic creativity.

The first sign of trouble appeared on the Sunday following moving day. Carol noticed her neighbor, Curtis Lanty, standing on his porch. He appeared to be in his early sixties and was wearing a sleeveless, dirty undershirt and wrinkled slacks.

"Good morning!" called Carol.

Lanty said nothing, but stared intensely at Carol while puffing on a cigarette. She developed goose bumps as she thought, this guy is a creep! Her instincts told her to avoid him as much as possible.

With each passing day Carol found new ways to add her unique style to the duplex. She planted a flower garden in the side yard and put up a birdhouse which she had painted to look like a brick building. A tiny sign above the entry to the birdhouse read: "Wills Creek Artists

Society." As she stepped back to assess her handiwork, she coughed at the smell of cigarette smoke. Turning, she saw Lanty standing on his porch, just a few feet from her. Again, he stared menacingly without saying a word.

Carol stomped into her apartment, slamming the door after her.

"That guy is not normal!" she said aloud.

Following an evening meal of frozen pizza and bagged salad, Carol sat on the couch with her sketch pad propped on her knees. Earlier in the day she had been to a farmers' market and thought some of the sights she had seen there would make good projects. She first sketched an elderly woman sampling pumpkin bread, then sketched a basket of tomatoes. Soon the pad became a picture book of various sights available only to small town observers.

Where did the time go? Carol thought, looking at the clock. It's dark already.

Carol put aside the sketch pad, stood and stretched her arms over her head. She approached the lamp on the stand by the window and, while reaching for the switch, noticed a small orange light outside. When the lamp turned off, Carol immediately saw the source of the mysterious light. Curtis Lanty was standing on his porch, smoking a cigarette and looking directly at Carol in her living room.

"That pervert could have been watching me for hours!" she fumed while yanking the curtains closed.

She tossed and turned throughout the night, her anger intensifying. Somehow she finally drifted into an unsettled sleep, but awoke two hours later. "I've got it!" she shouted as she sat up in bed. "I'll teach that freak to stare into MY window!"

Carol threw on some clothes and drove to Walmart. She bought a white window shade large enough to cover the entire window with an inch or two to spare. She laughed while driving home. "Wait until he sees this!"

Once home, Carol unrolled the window shade upon the newspaper-covered floor and brought out her paints. "This will be my best work ever!"

For the next couple hours, Carol worked feverishly. At last the masterpiece was complete. It dried quickly with the help of an electric fan. She was alive with anticipation as she installed the hanging brackets, then put up the shade. Giggling like a child on Christmas Eve, she returned to bed to wait for daylight.

Carol was not quite fully awake when she heard, "What the hell!" from her neighbor's porch. She grinned without opening her eyes and continued to enjoy the comfort of her bed.

Twenty minutes later, someone knocked on the door. Carol, assuming that it must be Mr. Voyeur, hastily dressed and half-combed her hair. She opened the door, prepared to give the creep a piece of her mind, and—good gracious, it was a cop! "Is there a problem, sir?" she asked in a tone much meeker than the one she was prepared to use.

"Sorry to bother you, ma'am, but your neighbor has reported that you have something obscene in your window."

Carol stifled a laugh and replied, "No, sir, just my personal artwork. Come this way and I'll show you."

As she led the officer to the side of the house, she noticed his muscular arms and summer-sky blue eyes. She also observed the lack of a ring on his left hand. Carol mentally kicked herself for not putting on make-up that morning.

"Here is the window," Carol pointed.

The officer's eyes widened, then he slapped his knees while erupting into uncontrollable laughter. There, painted on the window shade, was a five-feet-long reproduction of Curtis Lanty, complete with dirty undershirt, wrinkled slacks, unshaven face, and a cigarette.

"I don't think that is obscene, but it certainly isn't pretty," said the officer between episodes of laughter.

Lanty, on his porch during this time, threw his cigarette onto the lawn and stormed into his house.

Carol told the officer about her leering neighbor and how she had decided to give him something to stare at. "I'm sorry for your trouble, officer," she apologized.

"Oh, it's no trouble at all. By the way, my name is Jim and I'm an art lover, too. Monet is my favorite. Would you care to have dinner with me tonight and we can talk more?"

"I'd like that," replied Carol. "Besides, I don't want to be charged with resisting an officer."

SAMUEL D. BESKET

ALEX THE AX

After 40 Years He Got to Say Goodbye

Reading the morning paper with his wife was police detective Sgt. Don Barlow's favorite time of day. Although the TV was tuned to Fox News, they paid little attention to it as they chatted about current events.

When a news bulletin flashed across the screen, Don looked over the top of his glasses to read the crawler. Seeing that Alex Budskie, alias Alex the Ax, had walked away from a prison hospital ward, Don laid down his paper and turned his attention to the TV.

The crawler read how Alex, a trustee working in the hospital ward of Wills Creek Prison had walked away from the facility the previous night. State and local law enforcement officers were scouring the area looking for him. Residents in the vicinity of the prison were advised to stay indoors until he was captured.

Serving a life sentence for murder, Alex was considered a model prisoner. With skills acquired as a Marine medic during the Vietnam War, he had been assigned to the prison ward to work with terminally ill prisoners.

Alex drew national attention in the late 60's for the brutal ax murders of three men who had raped and murdered his wife. Following the murders, he walked into Detective Don Barlow's office, with blood-stained hands, and confessed to the crime.

Convicted and sentenced to life in prison, Alex's only request was to visit his wife's grave. Due to the viciousness of the murders and the amount of publicity surrounding the case, the judge denied his request.

Walking to the garage to retrieve the 40-year-old copy of Alex's file, Don's mind drifted back to the incident. He couldn't understand what motivated Alex to escape after all these years. He had appeared resigned to the fact he would spend the rest of his life behind bars.

Dusting off the file; Don sat in his restored 66 Mustang, and began to read the file. The facts became clear as he refreshed his memory. In their zest to capture the three suspects, police violated their Miranda Rights. Defense attorneys successfully convinced a judge to dismiss the case. Later that evening, celebrating their dismissal at a local tavern, the three suspects became boisterous and quite inebriated. Staggering from the bar in the early morning hours, they were confronted by an ax yielding Alex. The report described how he systematically dismembered the men.

Leaning back in the seat, Don recalled how contrite Alex was during the trial. His only outburst came when he was denied his request to visit his wife's grave. Scanning through the files, Don spied an old yellow newspaper photo of Alex's wife's funeral. A slight smile crossed his face as he read the details.

Dressing quickly, Don retrieved his badge and .38 police special from the gun safe. He backed the Mustang out of the garage replaying in his mind the events of that fateful day 40 years ago. Cruising quietly through the back entrance to Northwood Cemetery, Don parked in the shade of an old oak tree.

Walking up the hill, he quickly located Mary Lou Budskie's grave. Sitting on a stone opposite the grave, Don smiled at Alex. Looking up with tears in his eyes, Alex said. "They wouldn't let me go to her funeral, not even a visit to her grave. It was forty years ago today; I just had to visit her.

"I know, I know," Don said, gently putting his hand on Alex's shoulder.

A few minutes later Don spoke softly to Alex, "It's time we started back; your friends in the ward will miss you." Don pointed to the Mustang under the oak tree. "We better go. My car is just down the hill."

Driving up to the back gate of Wills Creek Prison, Don flashed his badge and was waved through by the guard. Stopping outside the back entrance to the hospital ward, Don shook hands with Alex.

"It might be better if you walked in by yourself, I'm going to put in a word for you with the warden. He's an old friend of mine. Anything else I can do for you, Alex, any questions?"

"Only one, Detective, only one." With a wide grin on his face he responded, "They must not pay you guys very much seeing how you still drive a 40-year-old car."

With that said, Alex turned and walked toward the prison door.

MARILYN DURR

Broiling Encounter
An Environmentalist, Unexpected Company And a Fire

Don Swanson, an environmentalist, stared toward a smoke-hidden horizon. It was impossible to tell the ravaged and smoldering Salt Fork State Park forest from the skyline. He'd spent a rough three days fighting this fire. Now it appeared under control unless wind direction changed and anticipated rains skirted the area. One never knew for sure how elements of nature would behave. Rain was a double-edged sword needed to help smother remaining flames, but if a downpour occurred, contaminated run-off would dump into Wills Creek and Salt Fork Lake causing huge fish kills.

Don knew it'd be up to him to get the ball rolling concerning reclamation efforts. *I need to rest, put food in my body... sleep, I need sleep.* His black hair frizzed in all directions as he shook his head trying to clear out mental cobwebs.

He trudged to a soot-covered white truck, his feet feeling heavy. *A baby learning to walk has an easier time staying upright.* His weary mind worked overtime sorting out thoughts. *I hardly have enough strength to open the door.* Don closed his eyes, resting his head on the steering wheel a moment. Then he started the truck and headed down a dirt service road to his camp. Darkness moved in early. Heavy smoke hanging in the air like black-out curtains blocked the last rays of the setting sun.

Pulling into camp he noticed a blazing campfire, "What's this? I doused and raked the coals this morning, how did... it... flare... up... again...?" His words trailed off when movement beside the tent drew

BROILING ENCOUNTER   **53**

his attention to a dark figure crouched over what looked like a cooked rabbit stretched out on a log.

"What are you doing here? Who are you? You're in a restricted area, there's a forest fire." He stepped closer. The figure stood, or rather uncoiled, to an astounding height and walked toward him with an outstretched hand. A webbed hand— with three large fingers and a thumb. A huge, pointed head sat on drooping shoulders with no visible neck. Eyes were positioned on the side of a scaly face in front of where a human's ears are placed. Permanently bent knees and colossal webbed feet completed the picture.

I'm hallucinating! Don's thoughts raced. It's not human! He screamed, loud and long. The creature screamed. Stunned, they stared at each other.

"Sorry, old man, I didn't mean to scare you. I was hungry, so I roasted a slogbot— rabbit in your language. Care to join me?"

It's a male voice, Don decided. "Well... sure." He figured it couldn't hurt.

"I'm known as Bilzup. My mother planet is Slipshod. What are you called?"

"Don." He wiped a stream of cold sweat from his forehead as one drop fell from the end of his nose. It sounded like a gong when it hit the soft forest litter, causing him to flinch.

"Well Don, I'm sorry about this mess I caused." Bilzup waved a webbed hand toward the smoldering forest, a frown creased his scaled face.

At least Don took it to be a frown. "You started the fire?" he asked.

"It was accidental, and am I ever embarrassed. My Wings backfired."

"Your—wings—backfired?" Don didn't see wings on Bilzup anywhere.

"My jalopy. I was cavorting around your galaxy in my reconditioned antique Wings spaceship when it ran out of fuel. It sputtered to Earth and gave a mighty backfire, starting a blaze. I managed to glide into a protected area surrounded by boulders. Then I found your home."

"Campsite." Don corrected. "It's not my home, it's a campsite. A temporary place to eat and sleep until the fire's out."

"Well, it's nice. Cozy." Bilzup placed his hands on his elongated hips, glancing around the camp. "Could use a little color here and there. Everything's gray and black. Somewhat dusty. You should clean."

"Bilzup, this place is gray and black and dusty because you burned the smithereens out of it! That's why there isn't any color. You made this mess, you clean it up." Don was bouncing like a jackrabbit jumping over prickly cacti, his contorted face turning bright crimson.

"Are you agitated, Don? Would you like a piece of roasted slogbot fur? It's tasty. Tickles when it goes down."

"You need to go home. Hitchhike if you're out of fuel—just go home," Don yelled as he shoved a finger into Bilzup's stomach. "What kind of fuel does your heap use? Plutonium? Nuclear waste? Hydrogen? What?"

"Mass-o-line, a powdered fuel hard to find on Slipshod. It hasn't been used much for over a century. When the governing body forced spaceship manufacturers to build more fuel efficient ships, mass-o-line production came to a near halt on planets with deposits of mass crystals," Bilzup sighed. "It wasn't cost effective after wealthy currency mongers started betting on sales and uses for the raw form."

"Bummer." Don said.

"Yes, quite profitable for them, but everyday planet dwellers went broke just flying to work." Bilzup shook his upper body, wiping a tear from his elbow tear duct with a long fingernail endowed appendage stuck on the end of his webbed hand.

"Exactly how does a dry powder fuel work? Combustion engines on Earth require a vaporizing liquid we call gasoline. It comes from refined crude oil."

"I know. Earth's a mandatory course for every Slipshodite. It's a continuing educational study so our planet doesn't become another goof-off-orb like Earth."

"Hey, I resent that statement," Don yelled. He was belly to—belly?—with the eight-foot alien and feeling the size of a sugar ant standing on the top rung of a six-foot step-ladder. His five-foot eight-inch stature seemed inadequate as he stared boldly into Bilzup's right eye. He would've stared into both if they'd been on the front of the extraterrestrial's face like any other beings' eyes, but since they weren't, one would have to do.

"You're on my lowest parts."

"What?" Don asked, his fury snuffed in mid-confrontation.

"My lowest parts—uh—my feet. You're standing on my feet. It hurts. On Slipshod it means we're engaged. Are we engaged? I-don't-think-so." Bilzup sounded worked up.

"Don't be huffy. I'm sorry. Now get back to your mass-o-line description."

"It's hostile to our environment's atmosphere they said. Weird thing, though, we could ingest it safely if we had the nerve. Hot water is added to the powder and stirred until it dissolves, then cold water is added. It's poured into the ship's tank before solidifying. It jiggles and has different colors. Brave Slipshodites who tasted mass-o-line say it comes in assorted fruit flavors."

"Jello? You're talking Jello? We got plenty of Jello on Earth. All kinds of flavors, too." Don clapped his hands. A huge smile slithered across his face. "You'll be home in no time, Bilzup. How much cash you got on you, buddy?"

"I'm not contagious and I don't have googlics on my person!" Don noticed Bilzup's right eye flashed anger, the left one looked the other direction, not wanting to get involved, he supposed.

"No, no, nothing like that. Cash is exchanged for Jello. It isn't free, you know. What are googlics?"

"Bugs, much like your fleas—only worse. I don't have your currency, either."

"How much Jello do you need? It comes in little boxes containing three ounces of powder." Don's excitement had him animated, bouncing up and down, waving his arms and grinning from ear to ear.

"It takes 12 of your ounces to fill the Wings' tank. But I still don't have your medium of exchange, old man."

"Stop calling me old man. You're not English, you're alien—like E.T. If that's all the Jello you need, I'll buy it. You stay here and get the water boiling. Fill this big pot to the brim. I'll be back in a jiff."

Bilzup ignored the E.T. slam.

When Don returned with the Jello, Bilzup had the water ready. Don, always thinking, bought a dishpan to mix the mass-o-line in and a large funnel to pour the fuel in the spaceship's refrigerated tank. It was tricky carrying liquid to the Wings over rocky terrain without spilling it, but they finally reached the spacecraft.

"What in the world! Your Wings is a 1950's era Ford Thunderbird," yelled Don. "How... where... a spaceship?" He sputtered. "When did Thunderbirds become spaceships?"

"Centuries before they were cars on Earth. They used to be our mode of transportation on Slipshod. You surely don't think Henry Ford came up with the idea on his own. We taught him everything he knew, but not all we knew. It was a trade-off. He didn't talk about us and we gave him plans for building automobiles. Sans space travel capabilities, of course. Simple, but it worked."

"She's a beauty," Don said as he held the funnel for Bilzup.

"She is, isn't she? My mate got upset when I bought her. She accused me of being in my fourth reptilehood. Didn't telepathy for two weeks."

"Yeah. They try to make you feel guilty, want you to think you did something criminal," Don said. "Your mate will never let you live this down."

"What I don't telepath to her won't hurt me, friend." Bilzup emptied the last of the fuel into his jalopy. "I better hit the galaxy. The mothership's waiting at the end of your cosmos for my transport back to Slipshod, but I'll come back to visit Cambridge and Wills Creek one day."

"I'll keep a stash of Jello on hand, buddy. Just don't burn down Salt Fork State Park's forest."

With that, the Wings Thunderbird lifted from the ground and turned west.

A loud whirr, a crack and Bilzup disappeared into the heavens.

"Wait," Don yelled, waving his arms wildly. "How do engines run on Jello?"

RICHARD A. DAIR

THE LAST STRAW
Someone Was Going To Die Before Sundown

This is a story of corruption in the early days of the American west. The two main characters are both men of low moral character. Tom, however, in the end, fighting personal demons, finds reason to stand up to his evil boss Flanagan. For the first time in his life he did the right thing.

Tom Cooper was suddenly awakened by the loud pounding on his hotel room door. "Mr. Cooper get up, Flanagan wants you down at his office pronto. Mr, Cooper, did you hear me?"

Tom reached for his gun. Promptly firing a round through the top of the door. "Does that answer your question, you little weasel?"

There was no reply, only the sound of boots racing down the hall. Should have aimed lower he thought. He hated that little bastard. Now awake, he became aware of the thunderous hammering in his head. A hangover, a bad one, even his joints were stiff. Opening his eyes only brought more suffering, small red spots swam across his vision like scum in pond water.

His final whiskey, the night before, a double, had been no different than the ten previous ones. But it went down reluctantly. Lately no amount of drink could wash away the demons that held his mind captive. What he was, and is, what he had always done for a living, now haunted his conscience.

In the beginning, the drinking eased what had always been expected of him. Now, no amount of rotgut could make his past or present go away. He's grown older and his evil deeds now enveloped him day and night. How much longer could he go on? It was eating him like a cancer. Tom knew he was already dead on the inside.

He had worked for men like Flanagan his entire life. Parasites they were, feeding on the meek and unfortunate. At first it was easy, and the money was good. There was no back-breaking labor, all that was needed was a fast gun. Having a reputation as a quick gun was a real asset. He was one of the fastest.

Most pilgrims that followed the wagon train west were dirt farmers. The only thing they ever fought were stubborn stumps and ornery mules. Not really much of a challenge for a man like himself.

Still fighting the pain in his head, Tom made his way to Flanagan's office. Would today be the day he stood up to him and walk away? Or would he do like he always did, back down?

Entering Flanagan's office, he pulled up the worn horsehair chair. Flanagan was already sitting in his new leather chair behind the desk. Tom looked directly into the cold grey eyes, damnable eyes he knew so well. He could easily read the thoughts and motivation behind them, greed.

It was always the same with men like Flanagan. They usually owned everything of value in the area, but always wanted more. More power, more land, they were insatiable.

Without speaking, Flanagan slid a paper in front of Tom. Tom knew what to do. It wasn't the first, and probably not the last time, one of his employers fancied a piece of property someone else owned. Honest people don't sell land they put their blood, sweat, and tears into, no, they have to be forced. Tom was the force. Just once he wished they would take the paltry sum that was offered and just clear out. But that never happened. And now the whiskey had no effect.

His eyes still bleary from the night before, Tom took the paper without looking at it. It didn't matter anyway. Some poor bastard was going to die, and he would wind up at the saloon downing doubles. Why hadn't he stood up to him today? What was it going to take?

He finished saddling his horse at the livery stable, checked his guns and for the first time, attempted to read Flanagan's paper. Who would it be today? Tom instantly became sober as he read the name. Something stirred deep inside his bowels. A primal sensation surged through his veins.

"No, not this time, not her," he screamed. He was livid as he burst into Flanagan's office to throw the paper on the desk. Tom's eyes red with fire.

"Why her," he demanded. "Her property is of no value to you."

Tom had often entertained the idea of courting the fine lady Becky Bradshaw himself, but realized she would probably have nothing to do with the likes of him. She and her husband, Joe, had been there only a short time when Joe mysteriously went missing. That was a year ago.

"I don't want her property, you damn fool, I want her," Flanagan shouted back " I've waited a year since I got rid of that husband of hers. Now I plan to move in." That was typical, the only way a man like Flanagan could acquire anything was through force and manipulation. Now that poor Joe's bones were bleaching out somewhere in the desert, all Flanagan had to do was sit back and wait. Destitute, Becky would be vulnerable, then when he thought the time was right he would move in like some sort of savior. More like the devil. This was the last straw. This was not going to happen. Tom found his courage.

Flanagan, realizing Toms intentions, reached for the derringer in his vest pocket. No one talked to him like that, not even Tom. Flanagan fired both barrels. Tom looked down, gut shot. The small caliber bullets usually weren't that effective, but at close range, a gut shot was usually fatal. Tom knew his time was short. He looked at the man who had been his employer just a few moments before, and grinned.

"What the hell you grinning at, you damn fool? Don't you realize you're a dead man."

"Sure I do, Tom smiled.,"

"Then what's so damn funny?"

"Nothing much, except I have six bullets left. See you in hell, Flanagan." With that, Tom pumped all six of the .45 five long Colts into Flanagan's chest before he hit the floor. When the smoke cleared both men lay dead. It was finally over. Soon a crowd began to form outside Flanagan's office, curious to see what happened.

In the crowd was Becky Bradshaw. She would never know just how lucky she was that day.

DICK METHENY

LOVE AT FIRST SIGHT
Was It True Love Or Just A Flash In The Pan?

What is it in a glance that can cause two people to fall in love without even a word being spoken? Rhonda and three of her friends from work were doing the girl's night out thing. Every Thursday night they got together and went barhopping. Typically, they would hit two or three places with live music then call it a night.

Harvey's was their second stop of the night. It was one of those places that changed its name regularly. This week the neon sign on the front of the building flashed Wills Creek Tavern. Next week it might be something else, but everyone still called it Harvey's. Featuring live music seven nights a week, the bar drew a good crowd during the week. It was always packed to the rafters on weekends.

Rhonda looked up from the table where she sat with her friends and saw him stop in the doorway to look around the room. His eyes met hers for only a few seconds but she knew instantly it was the real thing. She had been in love before, but it had not affected her like this.

Rhonda's gaze followed him as he moved to the bar. He certainly wasn't your classic soap opera idol, but good looking just the same. His curly blonde hair, blue eyes and easy way of walking sent chills up her spine. When she saw him smile at Gina, the barmaid, Rhonda was instantly jealous.

She hadn't noticed anyone coming in with him, maybe he was meeting someone. How could she get to meet him? What was his name? Why was she acting like a schoolgirl with a crush?

In all her 25 years no man had ever made her feel like this. She had to force herself to turn her head to keep from staring at him. She tried to listen to what her friends were saying, but all her attention was focused on a particular bar stool clear across the room.

Her mind raced to find a way to get to meet him. Would Gina know his name? It was worth a try. When Rhonda saw Gina lock her register to head for the ladies room, she grabbed her purse and hurried after her. She was coming out of a stall when Rhonda walked in. Gina washed her hands and stood in front of the mirror fluffing her hair. Rhonda got out her tube of lipstick and touched up the color on her lips then casually asked, "Hey, who is the blonde guy that came in a little while ago? I haven't seen him here before."

"Oh, that's Ray something. I forget his last name, but he is cute. He has only been in a few times. I've never seen him hit on anyone. I did hear him say he works just down the street somewhere. He never stays long, just a couple of drinks, listens to the music a little while and then leaves."

"Could you introduce me? You know, just in a casual sort of way?" "Honey, I can introduce you just as casual as all get out. But be careful, because I don't know this guy all that well. There's all kind of nutcases running around out there looking just as good as can be."

"I'm just curious about him. I'll be careful. Thanks, Gina, I owe you one."

"Just don't blame me if he turns out to have a wife and six kids."

When the barmaid left, Rhonda waited a few minutes before following her. Her eyes automatically went to the place he had been sitting and then she stopped in her tracks. There was a redheaded bombshell seated next to him talking a mile a minute. Damn!

Gina caught her eye and shrugged. As Rhonda walked toward the couple seated at the bar, his eyes met hers for just a few seconds. Again she felt that electrical current run all through her body. She was directly behind them when she heard him say, "Hell, Sis, I told you to cut that jerk loose a long time ago."

Sis! Sister! Thank you, Lord! Relief flooded over Rhonda as she returned to the table where her friends were seated. Her mind raced almost as fast as her heart. How could she meet this guy without seeming too forward? There had to be a way.

While the band was on break, Gina was too busy to even look

up let alone introduce her. Although she tried to talk them out of it, Rhonda's friends wanted to go to a place they had heard about across town. She was tempted to let them go without her but that wouldn't be polite. As the four of them headed for the door she caught Gina's eye and shrugged.

Rhonda came in every night for ten nights and he never showed up. She gave it up as a lost cause. When she stopped there on a Friday night, Gina said he had been in two nights in a row. He said he had been out of town on business. Damn! Just her luck! He had shown up the two nights she had not been there. Enough of this subtle crap, the very next time she saw him she was just going to plop herself on his lap and hope he didn't drop her on the floor. Well, maybe nothing that drastic. But she was getting a little frustrated after all this time.

This love at first sight thing could be good, but the logistics still needed fine tuning. Well, it was time to hit the road. Maybe she would run into him tomorrow night. She left Gina a tip, gave her a wave goodbye and headed for the door. Just as she reached the door, it opened and he walked in.

He held out his hand and said, "Hello, my name is Ray. I have been trying to catch up with you for two weeks."

Ray and I will have been married 10 years next month. I still don't know what was in that first glance that brought us together. I just know, whatever it is, we've still got it.

DONA McCONNELL

Lion's Share

How The Stars Ruled A Woman's Fate

As she closed the door behind her latest customer, Leona smiled. "What a chump," she thought to herself. He wasn't even suspicious when she snuggled close to him before he left, purring sweetly in his ear. As he beamed, her nimble fingers easily slipped the wallet out of his back pocket.

Leona had learned from experience not to take the goods too early. A couple of times, a guy had actually decided to give her a tip and reaching for his absent wallet had required some quick song-and-dance on her part.

Nobody fooled her now. She was a total pro. Her mother had always told her she was smart, with looks to melt men's hearts. She'd be rich someday, her mother promised – rich and beautiful. "You couldn't be anything else," her mother had had Leona. "You're a Leo – the sun sign – the most powerful sign in the Zodiac." It was true; no sign was stronger. The ruler of the planets. That's why she'd included Leona's sun sign in her name.

"Leona, you've got the power," her mother would say. For her 16th birthday, her mother had given her a gold chain with a lion pendant. The good looks were provided by her mother, she thought as she glanced at the mirror. Her mousy brown hair had been grown long and heavily streaked with blond – like a lioness, Leona thought – and her deep brown eyes gave her a brooding look that made men swoon. She'd used both to good advantage.

"Grrrrrrr!" Leona growled at the mirror. The Lioness at work!

Sounds in the hallway brought her back to reality. Time to move. She made a point of leaving the room quickly. There was always the chance the chump would miss his wallet before he left the hotel and she had to be long gone by then. Her car was always parked by the back entrance for a quick getaway.

As she fled down the interstate towards her brownstone in the city, Leona thought about her life. Sure, it wasn't what she'd planned. The problem had been that Leona believed her mother and thought the "magic" her mother had promised would just happen. Truthfully, Leona hadn't done much to create opportunities. Her mother had sacrificed to send her to one of the finest colleges, but she was an unenthusiastic student, majoring more in boys than her studies. Her datebook was always filled, one a senator's son whom her mother championed, but he was dull and unadventurous and Leona was easily bored. None of the goofy college guys were exciting enough for the life she had planned.

Then she met "the one" – Franklin, a rich, handsome blueblood from Connecticut. She was smitten, for once, as much as he was. They were inseparable and soon were talking about marriage. That's when Franklin's parents discovered their affair. It turned out, she may have been Franklin's type, but definitely was not his family's. At first she laughed off their objections but, unbelievably, Franklin followed their orders and dumped her. She was in shock; she phoned him, waited outside his dorm, and begged him to reconsider. Although he was obviously distraught as well, he explained that his parents would cut him out of their will if they married. It was all about the money. Even though Leona had to admit Franklin would lose some of his luster without his millions, she was devastated.

That was when life taught her its first hard lessons. You don't always get what you want; things don't always turn out the way you'd planned; and it's all about the money. Her mother had convinced Leona that life was hers for the taking. Franklin's rejection made her realize that money made everything different. She had never been rejected – it was Leos who rejected others, not the opposite. Her lost love and his attached fortune brewed bitterness in Leona's heart like a coffee pot brewing its morning potion. Leona became a different person – harder, colder, less like a sweet cub and more like an adult lion stalking its prey. A man-eater.

It didn't take long to realize she could make her own money. Good money. She found new, less savory uses for her natural assets. She started out small, in innocuous hotels in out-of-the-way places. Her uncle, to amuse her, had taught her the art of pick pocketing when she was just a child. This was quickly added to her portfolio of skills and her biggest take came from the wallets and gold watches she collected on her "evenings out."

Her business grew as she used her charm to become acquainted with the concierges of all the finest hotels. Soon her business, as well as her home, had moved uptown. She was able to afford a brownstone on 61st and the kind of clothes that enhanced her appeal to rich executives with discriminating taste and wallets to match.

The Francois Hotel was on a big-name street on the Upper East Side. It was a quaint old European style hotel with cobblestone streets surrounding it. Leona had made a particularly big score and was anxious to get home and put the cash in her private safe.

What a stupid lug this guy had been, a Wall Street type who thought he was doing her a great big favor. Egos! The rich guys were the worst, trying hard to be daring but scared to death of being found out. Not because of their wives; it was their precious six-figure jobs they valued so dearly. Careers clearly trumped marriages.

Leona had to admit that she was growing tired of her secret life. Her neighbors at her upscale condo thought she was an analyst at a brokerage house downtown. Years ago she had told her family she worked as a clerk at a large department store. As her wealth rose, she'd had to adapt her story to include ever-increasing promotions and bigger titles. Her mother, thank God, had left her at a young age and had never known what her "special" daughter had become.

It was a life of lies and Leona was tired. Maybe she'd think about a change, move to a new city, start a new life, a good life.

Thoughts of new places and faces filled her mind as she left the hotel. Outside, Leona picked up her pace. She had parked on a remote side of the hotel rather than wait for the valet. She was running late, and the Wall Street guys were always on tight schedules. Or at least they pretended to be. They thought a hectic schedule made them seem more important.

Rushing down the cobbled street, the spiked heel of Leona's designer shoe caught in a crack in the cobblestone walk. The shoe remained stationery, but Leona went flying feet-first into the air. She barely felt the smashing of her head against the edge of a half-full garbage can. The wound was minor, but the blow knocked her out cold.

Returning to consciousness several minutes later, moaning, Leona wondered what had happened. She couldn't see much in the dark alley and she couldn't seem to focus her thoughts. Wedged between two trashcans, she could barely move.

Suddenly, an alley cat jumped lightly onto her chest, a yellow tabby with long hair and golden eyes.

Leona's didn't see an alley cat. Her confused brain said was being attacked – attacked savagely – by a large jungle cat. Her namesake. Even now, he had her pinned to the spot with his massive paws. Leona's mind couldn't understand how the lion could be here. But she couldn't really remember where "here" was.

The cat, attracted by Leona's sweet smelling perfume moved up her body and sniffed her neck.

"Oh my God," Leona's mind whirled. "He's going for my throat." The animal inched closer, and suddenly she felt a jarring heave in her chest, followed by excruciating pain. As her last thoughts drifted away, calmness came over her.

Of course it was a lion. Of course it was going for her throat. That's what lion's do. Why, it was a perfectly fitting death. A lion – king of the Zodiac. Just like the one on her necklace. Fierce and proud. And her, his queen.

Early the next morning, two detectives stood over the still body.

"What you got, Harry?" one said, warming himself with a sip of hot coffee.

"A hooker with a massive heart attack," he officer said. "Something you don't see every day."

"You gotta admit she's a beauty," the other officer said. "Classy, too. If it weren't for the concierge at the hotel, I'd never have figured her for a lady of the night."

"Just goes to show you never know. Destiny, I guess."

As they waited for the coroner's office to take the woman away, they noticed a half-starved alley cat perched on top of a trashcan.

"Hey, look, Frank. Poor little guy." The officer leaned over and handed a piece of his bagel to the hungry feline.

"Cute, though," the other officer said as the cat gobbled the bagel and begged for more. "Look at his coloring. Looks just like a little lion."

JERRY WOLFROM

Autumn of 1945
The Wills Creek Cougars Gave It All They Had

The recent run of cooler, fall evenings, with clear, brisk mornings, followed by mild afternoons takes me back to the fall of 1945 – 60 years ago.

As nature smiles upon this land, it's fair to say this old memory has been set to prancing like a colt in green pastures – and suddenly I am on my way to football practice at Old Cory High, that field of hard clay, weeds and gravel can never be erased from my mind.

Only a sophomore that year, I barely tipped the scales at 130 pounds.

I dangled over my shoulder a pair of high-top football shoes, newly cleated by Dirty Doc, the village cobbler for 85-cents. He threw in a pair of new laces and two coats of rich Neat's Foot Oil to ward off the inevitable dampness. The new cleats were paid for with wages earned in a Waldhounding pickle field. The rate was a dollar a day, plus all the navy beans, bread, potatoes and milk I could stow away at noontime.

There was a small pickle-packing plant near Wills Creek High, which accounted for the preponderance of pickles nurtured in the area. Farmers signed contracts in the spring, complained all summer, then delivered a healthy crop with reluctance in the fall. Those of us at the tender age of 15 who were able to negotiate a 10-cent an hour raise were quick to note that the farmers were the only ones in the area to drive around in Buicks only slightly smaller than a railroad car.

We also suspected they had beefsteak for supper when there were no hired high school boys around to clutter up the premises.

As for the Valley Pickle Packing Plant, the true indicator of its prosperity was evidenced by the extent of the aroma it produced. The reason I digress is to underscore the fact that there is nothing new under the sun, including tension between workers, producers and manufacturers.

It's difficult in this era of inflated corporate and athletic salaries to explain why football practice at a small village high school was so important, not only to the boys and the coaches but to the adults who paid the taxes to support the schools.

At Wills High, we had an identification problem. Experiencing a certain feeling of isolationism in those days, we needed something to brag about – like a championship. After all, Barnesville had its own weekly newspaper. New Concord had a college employing 50 people, and Caldwell had three restaurants and a pool hall.

We knew our pickle plant wasn't enough. We needed a symbol of excellence that would cast us into the same class as those fine communities. Ergo, our football team, the Snarlin' Cougars.

The squad was 20 strong that year, composed of both village boys and those from rural areas. Each fall we set aside our natural suspicions of one another for the sake of community welfare. No easy task because refinement was clearly on the side of we town lads.

After all, we enjoyed electricity and indoor plumbing. And telephones were no longer considered a luxury in our circle. We also dressed better, got haircuts fairly regularly and were Methodists. Several Catholic boys from the rural areas were descendants of coal miners and even spoke in broken English. So the United Nations didn't have a more tenuous beginning.

But Coach (that's what we called him because there was no higher honor in those days) knew his team, the community and the opposition. He knew we faced an uphill battle that fall of 1945, so he installed the Notre Dame box formation, made famous by the Four Horsemen. It featured some tumultuous shifting in the backfield and pulling guards and tackles to run interference. The volunteer fire department on its busiest day never seemed so frantically rushed or so much in danger of head-on collisions as we carried out our fakes.

But Coach was right. The Old Cory High football team of 1945 had the speed and the heart, but it wasn't enough. Barnesville finished with a 10-0 mark. New Concord went 9-1 and Even Caldwell won five games..

Still, we boys of the mighty Snarlin' Cougars, despite winning only one game, learned to love one another. The town and country kids called an end to the hostilities, and that very affection abides among our grandchildren to this very day.

RICHARD A. DAIR

A Woman of Courage
She Was A Pioneer With True Determination

This story is set during a time in Ohio before there was a Cambridge or a Guernsey County. But it represents the type of men and especially women it took to claim the land. Settling near what is now known as Wills Creek, the story focuses on just one woman's story of determination and true grit.

Jim Bishop and Francis Collingsworth were in the settlement of Marietta to purchase supplies they and the others needed for the long winter. The first winter away from the relative safety of the settlement.

They had been away nearly a week. It was a five-day trek on foot and with all their provisions purchased, including a mule, to carry it. They were anxious to head back. Except for Francis, who wanted to spend another day down on the docks browsing the makeshift saloons. Bishop nixed the idea, knowing how rowdy Francis got when he started drinking.

So with their list complete and packed, they headed north. It was toward the end of the first days travel when a voice called out, one they instantly recognized. It was Laura, the wife of one of the men in their group, who had stayed behind to dress the beaver skins.

She approached them, exhausted, telling them of the trouble occurring at the camp and the fate of their fellow adventures.

Bishop had his concerns about Laura in the beginning. Barely five feet tall, maybe one hundred pounds soaking wet, she wasn't like most women in the territories, more refined, dainty, a real looker. Long strawberry blonde hair cascaded down to a slim waist, eyes as blue as the sky, a voice so sweet songbirds stopped to listen. Bishop imagined her more at home in a fine mansion in Philadelphia, not in a cabin of logs and mud.

However she an Ben were determined to stake a claim in the new territory. In the past two years Laura more than proved her worth.

Bishop and his party had detached themselves from the relative safety of the settlement in Marietta to strike out on their own. There hadn't been any recent trouble with the Indians. Settlers were anxious to move on to claim some of this beautiful Ohio Valley as their own. The party included Edward Crawford, Francis Collingsworth, Pierre Du Mont and Benjamin Rawlings, who was accompanied by his wife, Laura and their children Ben Junior and Sally. Their mission was twofold. Trap beaver and carve out a new settlement north of Marietta.

The year before Ben and Laura built a small cabin close to Wills Creek. There, beaver were plentiful , the water clear and sweet, and the earth dark and good for planting With the cabin completed, Ben set about trapping. Laura and the children planted the first garden. Soon the others followed. The location was five days journey from Marietta.

The single men built huts in the style of the local Indians. Ben and his family shared the cabin with the others for meals and protection, and so far all had been peaceful. While Jim and Francis were away to fetch supplies, the other men hunted. Laura and her children had remained in camp to dress the skins and prepare the evening meal.

Suddenly Laura heard footsteps. Pierre Du Mont, pale and bleeding, staggered through the door. Savages had surprised the men, killing Edward and her husband. Du Mont barely had strength left to give his information before he collapsed . Fearing the worst for herself and her children, Laura knew her only chance was to get away quickly.

With presence of mind and force of character, she gathered some dried beaver meat and dried biscuits. She added her long knife. She knew it was only a matter of time before the savages would trail Du Mont back to the cabin. Finding a stout hickory stick, she fashioned a primitive crutch, gathered her children and began heading for the secret spot. A place prepared for just such an emergency. There, extra powder , a flintlock, and a spare canoe had been stashed.

The small group of survivors would hide and wait for Jim and Francis to return. She observed a number of Indians on horseback moving west toward her cabin, Her position was well concealed and they weren't spotted.

She and her children, slept without fire or water for two days; she kept the children warm in her arms. During the night she found poor Pierre had died. She hadn't seen any Indians for more than a day, however Laura knew they could still be there, waiting.

At dawn the next day, the resolute woman decided to continue on. Ten miles south another pioneer family had settled where she would seek refuge with them until the others returned. She would have to go slow. Indians could be anywhere. However she knew she had to do it. She couldn't risk burying Pierre, and the thought of staying with a rotting corpse was not a option. It had been three days since the attack.

Laura now found herself alone in the wilderness with two small children in tow. No food, only a single-shot flintlock for protection, facing the unknown with a savage enemy surrounding her. Her chances were bleak.

Ten miles equaled two days travel by foot. She strained her eyes, not wanting to be taken by surprise. Lack of food and sleep began to take its toll. In the early morning of the sixth day, tired and exhausted, Laura spotted smoke. They were near their destination and she hoped it came from a cook stove. Nearly starved, the thought of a proper breakfast invigorated her efforts.

The deserted building showed marks of blood from a terrible massacre. Smoke arose from the smoldering embers of the family cabin. Laura feared the entire family had fallen victim to the Indian attack. She turned in fresh horror and continued south. For two more days, she continued forward, ready to collapse for want of food, since she had given her children most of the berries, wild onions, and dandelion leaves they gathered along the way.

Still she forged ahead. It had been days since she saw any sign of Indians. Perhaps they were gone; perhaps they were waiting around the next bend. All she knew was that she had to lead her children to safety, even if it meant walking all the way back to Marietta.

74 THE WILLS CREEK CHRONICLES

At midday, she found herself near faint from exhaustion. It would have been so easy to just give up, to lay down, to sleep, but the thought of some savage raising her children kept her going. It was then she spotted Bishop and Collingsworth. Without hesitation, she gathered her children and the flintlock and stumbled forward calling out to them, excited to have found them, Laura didn't know whether to laugh or cry.

She seemed to do both as she began to explain to them about the Indians and what had taken place. Knowing she and her children were safe, Laura gave in to her exhaustion and slept.

For protection, Bishop, and the remainder of their party, decided to return to Marietta. After a few days, word reached them that the Indians were a band of renegades. They had been captured and hung. It was the last Indian uprising ever reported in the area.

Bishop and Collingsworth were anxious to get back to camp. Winter was approaching and they needed to prepare for the trapping season. It would be harder now that they were three men short.

"You weren't planning on leaving me behind were you?"

"Laura," Bishop gasped. "You can't be serious?"

"Serious as a toothache," she quipped. "That spot your heading for was Ben, and my dream. Nothings changed. Besides you'll be dead from food poisoning within a week if I don't."

"That's for sure," Collingsworth assured him. "Sorry, Jim, but you can't cook worth a damn."

"Then its settled, I'll fetch my children and my supplies. Meet you back here in ten minutes." With that said, she turned and hurried down the street.

"That's one hell of a women, Bishop said. "All one hundred pounds of her."

"Yeah, I feel safer now that she's coming," Collingsworth teased.

"Ah, shut up, and load the mule you damn fool."

For whatever reason , both men were happy she was going. It would be a good trapping season.

JOY L. WILBERT ERSKINE

THE DEAD GIRL NEXT DOOR
The Haunting of Highland Hills

Through the window of the taxi, Harry saw only a muddy field where the house he was looking for should've been. At the back of the lot, a trio of burnt oaks stood conspicuously alone, like naked soldiers on sentry duty.

An all-business, matter-of-fact working man, Harry didn't like surprises. "I'm in no mood for this," he fumed. He drove slowly forward to the next address. Peering through the drenching rain, he could see lights in a window. He snatched up the crumpled napkin he'd scribbled the address on and made a fast dash to the porch, but he got soaked anyway.

Carelessly brushing his hands down his jeans, he inadvertently squished rain into his sneakers. "Blast it!" he growled as the water sopped into his socks. He punched the doorbell and tried to summon up a smile as he listened for footsteps.

A feminine voice called, "Just a minute." A moment later the door opened quietly, revealing a middle-aged woman with her head wrapped in a towel. "Hello? May I help you?" she inquired.

"I hope so," Harry sighed with vacant optimism. "65585 Highland Hills Road, the Zimmerman house. That would be the empty lot next to you, am I right?"

The woman stepped onto the porch. "Yes, the house burned four years ago. Julie and Aaron moved, but they still tend the property." Wrapping her arms around herself, she sized Harry up and said, "Why don't you come in and get warm? I just put the coffeepot on. My husband, Amos, will tell you about the place." She glanced at the battered blue Ford. "Oh, are you holding a cab?"

"No, I'm the driver. Just on my way home and got a pickup call. You say a Julie Zimmerman lived there?" he asked, perplexed.

"Yep," she affirmed with a shiver. "Come in or we'll both freeze." She stepped back, holding the door open for him. "Amos! Company! Hang your hat there," she pointed, "and follow me."

She led the way to a cheerful country kitchen where a warm fire crackled in the hearth. Amos sat at a trestle table with the newspaper spread out before him. He quickly gathered it up and sprang to his feet to shake Harry's hand. "Hello! I'm Amos Kerrigan."

"I'm Teresa Kerrigan," the woman added. "And you...?"

"Harry Briggs. On my way to Antrim, just up the road a ways."

"Oh yes, we know it," Teresa grinned brightly. She pulled a third mug from a cupboard just as the coffeepot gurgled to a finish.

"Have a seat," offered Amos, waving toward a worn wooden rocker by the fire. "Looks like you need to warm up. Make yourself comfortable." Teresa carried steaming mugs to the table and set one close to Harry.

"What brings you here on such a miserable day?" Amos asked.

"If you'll excuse me," interrupted Teresa, "I'll go dry my hair. Take your shoes off and set them by the fire to dry," she suggested. Sliding a plate of cookies onto the table, she disappeared into the back of the house.

Harry turned back to Amos. "I came looking for the address next door, expecting find a house, not an empty lot. Your wife says the house burned?"

"Yeah, a horrific blaze. One minute the house was fine and the next it was an inferno. A fireball from heaven couldn't have obliterated it any faster," Amos shook his head in remembered wonder.

"Wow! How did I miss that in the Jeff?" Harry mused.

"The paper ran just a small article, at the family's request. It's no wonder you missed it. The Zimmerman's were devastated. They lost a daughter in the fire. She's buried under the oak trees. Why are you interested?"

Harry clamped his cold fingers around the coffee mug. "I don't really know." He explained, "I'm a taxi driver in Cambridge. Just finished my shift so, as usual, I stopped for a sandwich at the Main Street Café before heading home. Annajean Taylor, the waitress, told me the dispatch office called. I was to pick up a woman at this address. Said she specifically asked for me. Now I'm here and there's no such place. Seems pretty strange is all."

"Did she give her name?" interjected Teresa as she returned to the kitchen. "I'll check the phone book," she offered.

"Susannah Zimmerman."

Momentarily, the Kerrigan's gaped at him like possums caught in the headlights, then Teresa regained her composure. "There're probably lots of Susannah Zimmerman's. You just got the wrong address."

"Can't be that many, Teresa. Check the book," Amos suggested. "This isn't a big metropolis, y'know." To Harry, he expounded, "The only Susannah Zimmerman we know is the girl who died in the fire next door."

The room seemed to hold its breath while Teresa thumbed through the white pages. "…Zimmer, Zimmerly, Zimmerman," she mumbled. "Nope, only seven Zimmerman's, mostly female, but no Susannah."

The phone rang at Teresa's elbow and she jumped in spite of herself. Stammering, she answered, "K-Kerrigan's." Amos started to say something to Harry, but stopped cold when Teresa choked out, "Who is this?" He turned just as her face went pale and she dropped the receiver. He jumped to her side and grabbed the phone. "Who is this?" he shouted. "Talk to me!" He heard a click, then nothing but dial tone.

Amos hung up, cursing, and sat Teresa down gently. "You okay, honey? Who was it? What'd they say?"

"She said it was Susannah," whispered Teresa. "She wanted to talk to Harry." Her voice broke. "It sounded just like her, Amos. Just like her."

Harry sat in a daze, trying to take it all in. Amos turned to him, suddenly cold, and said, "You've got some explaining to do, mister. What's going on here?"

Harry about choked on his own spit. "Don't ask me. I don't even know this Susannah." A flash of inspiration hit him and he countered, "It's you two! You guys are trying to freak me out, aren't you? I'm getting out of here." He seized his shoes and started for the door.

The phone rang again and Harry stopped dead in his tracks. None of them could breathe or move. They stared at it as if it was possessed. After several rings, the answering machine clicked on. Wordlessly, they listened as the message and beep sounded. "This is Susannah. I just need to talk to Harry. I need his help. Pick up the phone. Now!"

With a nod, Amos motioned Harry to the phone. Harry trembled as he lifted the receiver to his ear. The answering machine continued to record. Amos and Teresa listened tensely. "He-ello," squeaked Harry weakly. "Who is this, really?"

"I'm Susannah Zimmerman, the girl who died in the fire next door. You know the man who killed me."

Harry jerked as if the phone had scorched his ear. Teresa gasped and fell against Amos. Harry croaked, "You got the wrong guy. Who are you? What do you want, really?"

"I only meant that you happen to know of him, Harry," Susannah said soothingly. "I want you to turn him in to the police. The evidence you'll need is in your pocket."

"What?!" Incredulous, Amos moved between his wife and Harry, producing a handgun out of nowhere. "Empty your pockets on the table," he directed.

Harry did as he was told. Two quarters, a bloody handkerchief, a pen, and his wallet tumbled onto the tabletop. "That's all I've got," he said, turning his pockets out. "Take it easy, Amos. I'm no threat to you."

"The handkerchief, Harry," Susannah interrupted icily. "Remember where you got it?"

"Annajean gave it to me when I nicked myself with a steak knife at the café."

"Are those her initials on the handkerchief, Harry?"

Harry fumbled with the handkerchief, looking for a corner with initials. "S.Z." Harry read the initials out loud. His skin crawled as fresh horror crept over him. "Susannah Zimmerman?" his voice wavered.

"Good, Harry. Now, why would Annajean have a handkerchief with my initials?" Susannah asked, as if quizzing an idiot.

"I don't know, Susannah. Tell me," Harry choked.

THE DEAD GIRL NEXT DOOR   **79**

"Because Ernie Taylor tossed it in the laundry. There was soot on his little souvenir. Annajean discovered it when she did the wash, so Ernie told her he'd found it in the café. And she kept it. This morning, she put it in her pocket before she left for work. Now, all I want you to do is deliver it and the answering machine tape to the police, Harry. They'll do the rest."

"But Susannah," Teresa found her voice, "why did Ernie kill you?"

"He loved me, Teresa. I turned him away and he went crazy. I was asleep when he set the house on fire. Poor stupid Annajean, living with that monster. I've been waiting for something to trip him up and now Harry's got the proof. At last, I can put this behind me and move on." Her voice tensed, "You will help, Harry. Or I can make you help, if you prefer. I have the power, you know." With that, a crackling "BANG" sounded in their ears and everything went black. Teresa screamed.

BEVERLY J. JUSTICE

THE GOOD BOOK
A Unique Solution From An Unlikely Source

The steady creaking of a rocking chair and gentle hum of an air conditioner were the only sounds in the small one-story house. Kate Blackthorne had endured the worst three months of her 72 years and relaxed in the feeling of serenity that enveloped her. The sadness, uncertainty, and anger that had occupied every minute of her recent days were finally gone.

When Frank Blackthorne retired seven years ago, he and Kate decided to sell their house and find a small rental near their hometown of Liberty, Texas. Their only child, Joseph, was a professor at Muskingum University in Ohio and encouraged his parents to find a home in which his father would have to do little maintenance. Although Joseph and Kate did not express their fears to Frank, both worried about his failing heart.

The rental house seemed to be the answer. It had only one floor, so there were no stairs to climb; the landlord, Ed Radnor, was prompt with all repairs and yard work. Neighbors were friendly but not intrusive. We were so happy, thought Kate as she rocked in the same chair in which she had rocked Joseph to sleep decades ago.

Every June Ed Radnor would bring the lease to the house for Frank and Kate to sign. He had raised the rent only twice in seven years and assured the couple the house would be theirs for as long as they wanted.

Then in April Kate's world fell apart. One morning while shaving, Frank complained of shortness of breath and a dull ache in his jaw. In spite of Frank's protests that he was fine, Kate called for the ambulance. Within two hours Frank was dead.

The following weeks were a blur. Joseph and his wife, Jenna, handled the funeral arrangements and stayed with Kate for a week. After they had returned to Ohio, Kate feared that she would become lonely and depressed. Surprisingly, she felt reassured in the familiar surroundings of the house and could sense Frank's presence. At times, she would even talk to him.

On Memorial Day weekend, a mere six weeks after Frank's death, the unthinkable happened. When Kate saw Ed Radnor approach her door, she assumed that he was bringing the lease for signing. Instead, Ed bluntly informed Kate that the lease would not be renewed. His divorced daughter would be moving into the house. Kate, and all her possessions, would have to be gone by the first of July. Kate cried and pleaded, but Ed was unmoved. He was sorry, he said, but family comes first.

Joseph made arrangements for Kate to move into Wills Creek Manor in Cambridge, only three miles from his home. Kate and Frank had been to Cambridge many times to visit Joseph and Jenna, and both loved the scenic town. But it was not home and Kate would never be able to cram all of her possessions into the apartment. Her heart broke when she was forced to sell the pine bookcase Frank had made with his own hands.

In the weeks following Ed's visit, Kate experienced emotions she did not believe she owned. She had never hated anyone in her life, but she hated Ed Radnor. In fact, she was consumed with hate. She found herself wishing he would crash his fancy truck into a ravine and crush his skull. She fantasized of a Texas twister picking up Ed and his daughter and slamming them head-first into a silo. Kate knew these thoughts were not constructive, but she did not know how to regain control of her life.

She received her answer from a source she had completely overlooked: Reverend Stanton. Usually his sermons were more soporific than inspiring, but on that particular Sunday his quote from the Bible hit Kate right between the eyes. The burden was lifted. She knew what she had to do.

The next day just before lunch Kate telephoned Ed to ask if he would like to have Frank's bowling ball. "I know you bowl in a league and I really don't want to take a 16-pound ball to Ohio," she told him. At first Ed stammered, as if he could not believe what he was hearing. But Kate's voice had been so kind and cheerful that he soon agreed to stop at the house and take a look at the ball.

When Ed's truck turned onto the driveway, Kate arose from the rocking chair and greeted him at the front door. "It's next to the tool shed," she smiled warmly. "It's too heavy for me to carry into the house."

Ed walked toward the back of the house and approached the shed. Outside the door was a blue nylon bowling bag with a black leather handle. Kate watched Ed from the screen door that separated the kitchen from the small back porch. Ed was impressed with the bag, nodding his approval. Kate smiled at him through the screen door. Ed squatted next to the bag to unzip it.

Springing from the bag, the reptiles were upon Ed in less than a second. The tan and bronze diamond patterns on their backs glistened in the sun as they fulfilled their deadly task. Kate was unable to see the actual biting or venom, but she was not disappointed with the results.

Ed jumped to his feet and covered his face with his hands. No use; he already had been bitten on the nose and left hand. Ed turned toward Kate. Even from that distance she could see that his nose was considerably swollen. He began to stumble toward the back porch. His left hand was twice its normal size and a deep hue of purple. The arm dangled uselessly as he staggered toward the porch.

From this distance Kate could see that Ed's face was no longer recognizable as that of a human being. His eyes were nothing more than slits and his nose now occupied his entire face. Just as he reached the steps of the back porch, he collapsed. Kate, still smiling, looked down upon the wretched man and recalled the words that Reverend Stanton had quoted that day from Proverbs 23:32: "At the last it bites like a serpent, and stings like a viper."

BARBARA KERNODLE-ALLEN

Was It Fred's Plan?
Three Hearts Are Mended

Two weeks after the funeral, Sarah, heart feeling like a stone in her chest, was still walking on legs made of lead. She took care of her mother through her final illness. They had been close. Perhaps it would have been easier if she'd had siblings. The loneliness was crushing. Completing the tasks automatically, Sarah paid bills, filled out insurance forms, and cleaned out her mother's apartment. Taking only a few treasured mementos, she packed most of the things to donate to Goodwill. Every item contained a memory, bringing a tear or a sigh.

Heading back to work, Sarah pulled the gray Honda Civic into a space in the far corner of the parking lot. Exiting the car, she felt she was being watched. Looking about, she saw him...a large black and white cat staring intently at her from a window in the duplex directly in front of her. His big green eyes were almost obscured by huge black irises. Reminded of a comical man in a tuxedo, she smiled for the first time in weeks.

Entering the office building, Sarah was greeted by co-workers offering condolences as they went about their business. Her first day back, catching up on e-mail, prioritizing the thousand and one tasks that needed done before tax time. Waves of overwhelming emptiness washed over her.

That evening, upon approaching her car, Sarah glanced at the window, looking for the cat. As their eyes met, his intent stare held her gaze. He placed a white gloved paw against the pane. A greeting?

84 THE WILLS CREEK CHRONICLES

A plea? "Did he want something?"

Sarah returned to her cold, lonely little house and the cold pizza waiting there. Uneasy thoughts kept drifting back to the cat in the window, disturbing her sleep, intruding into her dreams.

After a fitful night with little sleep, Sarah took the same parking place, wondering if the cat would still be in the window. Empty glass stared back at her. Disappointed, she started to turn away, when a movement caught her eye. Placing one white paw against the pane, he opened his pink lipped mouth. The glass muffled his plaintive cry.

Throughout the long day, the image of the tuxedo cat with his beseeching gesture haunted Sarah, but when she returned to her car, the window echoed emptiness... No cat...no curtains. Everything gone. She stood for a few moments, hoping, staring at the window. An elderly man opened the door, asking if she was interested in renting the apartment. Embarrassed, Sarah admitted she was hoping to see the cat.

"Oh... that one... No, he's not here. His owner had a stroke. Her son took her to Wills Creek Acres Nursing Home. The Humane Society took the cat this afternoon. They'll probably put him to sleep." Shocked, Sarah asked, "Why?"

"Well, he don't make up with most folks. He bit and scratched something awful when they came for him. He's a mean one," he said, shaking his head.

Sarah got in the car and left the old man standing in the doorway. As she drove out Old 21 Road toward her Northgate Addition home, she passed the bridge over Wills Creek, leading to the nursing home. Suddenly it hit her. She had to do something...but what? She slammed on the brakes and screeched to a halt. Clouds of dust and gravel flew at the entrance to the Fish Basket Storage business.

Trying to decide what to do, she wondered why the cat's fate disturbed her so much, about the old lady who had owned him, his vicious behavior, and most of all, his pleading gesture. Dogs barked and a man came around the building. She needed to leave.

Realizing she would never be satisfied until she checked on the cat, Sarah turned the car around, heading for the cat shelter. She told the volunteer she was interested in seeing the cat.

He warned her "it" was dangerous and had injured several people that day. Sarah promised to keep a safe distance.

There he was, huddled in a cage. Ears folded back. Tail twitching. Teeth bared. Claws out. The hair on his back spiked like a Mohawk. Feline hostility! Sarah wondered why she'd come.

The change was startlingly swift when he saw her. Jerking to attention, his ears pricked up and long white whiskers fanned forward. He tentatively extended a sheathed paw toward Sarah, opening his pink mouth to make a soft, questioning "mew?"

As she leaned forward to get a closer look, the cat began to purr. Sarah didn't hesitate to pop the latch and lift 15 pounds of fur, muscle, teeth, and claws into her arms. The volunteer gasped and moved to protect her. The big cat pressed his cold nose to her cheek, rubbing his face along her jaw. She giggled as she hugged the cat. "I'm taking him home."

Thinking to notify his previous owner that he was safely adopted, Sarah stopped at the nursing home the next afternoon. Greeted by a lady with a pleasant smile, Sarah explained she came to let a new resident know she had her cat. The staff was happy to know the cat was safe.

Edna had been fretting about him since the moment she'd arrived. She was thrilled to meet Sarah, telling her all about "Fred." "His name is Fred Astaire because he dances and leaps about in his tuxedo, chasing his tail."

Forging a friendship based on mutual loneliness and their relationship with Fred, who they agree is not owned by anyone, they look forward to Sunday afternoons together. Sarah takes Edna out to eat and to visit with Fred, when she is well enough. They laugh at Fred's antics, and wonder if he planned for them to meet. Fred, curled on his chair by Sarah's window, blinks and hides a smile behind his tail.

J. PAULETTE FORSHEY

MR. LAMBERT'S LIBRARY
One Man's Library Is Another Woman's Freedom

The house sat in an off corner of Cambridge, but then, houses like that always do. Houses such as that never are located in a conspicuous place in towns, but then maybe that's why they attract people like Lambert.

Oh, I digress, I must tell of the house first, for the house is what they saw in their daily lives.

The grounds were well kept for the most part, though some would argue that the hedge could have used a more defined clipping. But, it would not have hidden the rust-coated iron fence so well. Funny thing, that aged, pockmarked, rusted fence with its fixed-open gate and sections held up only by that hedge. It managed, still, to do its job, and do it well indeed. A patchwork stone path led to the once-elegant, wrap-around front porch while a muddy ribbon of Wills Creek ran behind the house. One could imagine fine ladies in pale gowns seated on white wicker, sipping lemonade while young gents sporting straw hats strutted among them in their Sunday best. One could imagine it, but then, no one could remember such an event ever occurring on that peculiar porch.

The windows remained closed, forever closed, even on the hottest, most humid days, like the eyes of a giant child slumbering peacefully in its mother's arms. But then, they only saw the outside of the house in their daily lives.

The day Mr. Lambert placed a notice on the post office bulletin board, he caused quite a stir. Well, not really Mr. Lambert himself, or not that they weren't used to seeing Mr. Lambert about town. It was just, well, Mr. Lambert was a meticulous man, and on that day, and until that very day, he was – well – rumpled.

His hair, a light maple brown, usually clean and combed just-so to one side, had not seen either soap or brush for several days. Mr. Lambert's fresh-pressed suit of rich English tweed, a suit that many described as making him dashing in a scholarly way, looked as though he'd worn it sleeping and awake. His necktie, once neatly knotted at his throat, was now non-existent, and his clean-shaven face now fostered a formless stubble.

Even his eyeglasses roosted at a precarious angle. Everyone was startled by his appearance, they didn't know about Mr. Lambert's library.

They gathered around to read the hastily scrawled notice:

WANTED:
INTELLIGENT, EDUCATED PERSON TO DO
RESEARCH AND CATALOGING OF RARE BOOKS.
MAN PREFERRED
(Quiet woman will be considered)
REPLY P.O. Box 1331

She arrived carrying a faded old carpetbag, a suitcase of sorts from yesteryear. Her dress, once brightly colored, now a pale ghost of itself, clung to her womanly figure, as stockinged legs swished rhythmically with each determined stride. Her face they never saw until – that – day for she wore a large-brimmed hat over long, confused auburn tresses. Where she had come from, or how she had gotten there, no one could say. Most remembered her steadily walking as though on an already fixed path to Mr. Lambert's front door.

Some stood on their porches, others trailed discretely behind to watch as she ascended Mr. Lambert's front porch steps. She placed the carpetbag down by her feet, and using the

88 THE WILLS CREEK CHRONICLES

brass pistol-knocker, struck the door twice, the sound echoing in the still, late-day air.

Mr. Lambert opened the door so that only half of his face could be seen. No one remembers hearing what passed between them. Mr. Lambert was seen shaking his head once in a negative way. She placed both hands on her hips, cocking her head to one side. Hesitantly, he opened the door wider. As she picked up her bag and strode in, he shut the door carefully. That was the last they saw of her.

Mr. Lambert made several trips downtown to buy paper, pencils, pens, folders and such things. Many tried to engage him in conversation about himself, or the young woman they'd seen, but not once would Mr. Lambert answer their queries. They watched and waited, waited and watched, and so did we.

Though Mr. Lambert found us first, he did not realize what we were, or what we could do; by the time he did recognize the power we possessed, it would be too late.

We are what is left of an ancient civilization. We are what is left of their words, thoughts, the very essence of their beings. We retain the power they once thrived on, and we need to thrive again in their world.

Mr. Lambert did not want her to come into his newfound world, but gently we whispered he must let her in. We explained that for every Yin there is a Yang. In this respect, the Chinese and Egyptians understood us best, but alas, even they did not understand us completely. Mr. Lambert read and re-read us. At first, after he whispered our words he did not fully make the connections as to what was happening around him. The evening he muttered the growing words, touched the lovely, bold iris, we hoped he would see in the morrow's morning light that which we could achieve. No, not even when we helped bring the cool, sweet breeze inside his cloistered home, he did not see or understand. Mr. Lambert in his cobwebbed mind only wanted to research and catalog us.

She came knocking at his door. She came, ripe within her the life we so needed, and we nudged him to look at her, to see her through our eyes. But then, Mr. Lambert was as blind as they were.

She did as he asked, cataloging us, but she also noticed what happened when he spoke our language. She asked him to teach her our language, to understand our purpose. It was then he began to lightly comprehend.

Like so many before him, sadly he chose to see us not as we truly were but through man's narrow, tunneled vision. Demons, he ranted of us. He tried to destroy us and when his attempt failed, he tried to lock us away. But she had touched us, she began to hear us, and now she felt our seductive caresses and wanted more, as we wanted her.

Outside they saw in their daily lives a quiet, darkened house.

Outside they shook their heads and whispered their many speculations of Mr. Lambert, the woman, and his library.

Outside they uttered trite concern, more curious conjecture. The fate of all – not two – was now at hand, they said.

They came into our lives; we tried to open that part of his mind that would save him, but then, he was more of them than us. The burly sheriff, crimson-faced in the midday heat, shook his head as they took Mr. Lambert away that day. They searched the house inside and out, never looking in the place they should for her. She was safe, nestled in our arms, bedded down between our creamy sheets. She would wait until we found her Yang.

Yes, they looked. Though they saw, they did not see.

We cried for Mr. Lambert, truly, we did. The burly sheriff that led him away kept saying how sad it all was. Poor Mr. Lambert sniffled, gurgled and laughed to himself, and repeated in a sing-song voice. He had warned her about the library; now it was too late.

SAMUEL D. BESKET

Final Meeting

He Finally Got To Speak To His Father

Walking into the kitchen Jeff saw the letter in the middle of the table. "It's from your brother John," his wife Mary said. "I hope it's not bad news."

"It's probably about Dad," he replied. "It's about the only time he writes." Jeff opened the letter while Mary poured him a cup of coffee.

"I know things have been strained between you two," the letter went on. "But, Dad is in Wills Creek hospital and I thought you might want to see him."

Strained. More like hostile, Jeff thought. Things never were good between me and Dad. I think he still blames me for mom dying when I was born.

Turning toward Mary, Jeff said, "I didn't know my father until I was five years old. I stayed with my grandparents until he married John's mom. When I did see him, he was always hard on me. Even after John was born I didn't see him much, he spent all his spare time with him."

During the drive to the hospital, Jeff relived many of the bad memories he had growing up. I don't know what good this will do, he thought. He never did want much to do with me or my family.

Pulling into the hospital parking lot Jeff recalled when John was born. He showed the baby to everyone, while I sat in a corner, he remembered. If it hadn't been for grandma they would have walked out and left me.

As Jeff walked into his dad's room John stood up, "He's not very responsive and the doctors don't know what's keeping him alive. I'll be outside if you need me."

Sitting beside his father's bed Jeff spoke. "I know things were hard for you when mom died. I thought you blamed me for her death. I didn't know what do," he replied, bowing his head.

Suddenly Jeff felt his father's hand on his arm. Looking up he saw his father smiling at him.

"Every time I looked at you I saw your mother and I blamed you for her death," his father said. "I want to make things right between us; I don't want you and your boys to remember me as a mean old man." With tears running down his cheek he asked Jeff to forgive him. "I did years ago, Dad, I did years ago."

Standing, he leaned over and kissed his dad on the forehead, "Sleep, Dad, you need rest." His dad was already asleep as he walked out of the room. Waving to John, Jeff left the hospital.

Pulling into the driveway, Jeff saw Mary standing on the porch. "The hospital just called. He's gone. He died shortly after you left."

"I know" Jeff said, "I know."

Hugging Mary, Jeff spoke. "Finally, after all these years I got to talk to my father."

DICK METHENY

Is Mike Regan Dead or Alive?
Does He Really Have Nine Lives?

Mike Regan got elected in a landslide victory by promising voters he would clean up the crime and corruption that was rampant in the city and county. John Q. Public believed him and voted accordingly. What made things even stickier was that Mike Regan believed it.

Mike was county prosecutor only six months before he indicted the county sheriff, three deputy sheriffs, the city police chief, two police captains and a judge for a long list of crimes. At the top of each indictment was bribery, abuse of power, extortion, negligence and malfeasance in office.

From this point, the charges varied according to what Mike could prove on each of the individuals. Three civilian city employees were also indicted. A special grand jury was seated to consider the charges and the news media was filled with speculation over what would happen next.

Almost immediately there were two separate attempts to kill Mike. The first was an amateurish attempt to make it look like a burglary gone bad. Regan easily disarmed the burglar and held him for the police. The second try was a drive-by shooting that only inflicted minor cuts to his hands and arms from flying glass and severe damage to his best suit pants as he dived behind a parked car.

When Mike promised reporters more arrests were coming, political factions threatened to unite and bring impeachment charges against him, but nothing ever came of the threats. No savvy politician ever wants to go on record as being against reform. That road leads directly to political suicide.

When several of the indicted individuals promised to sue him for slandering their good name, Mike held a news conference to announce he would challenge any of the parties involved to prove in court they even had a good name. This public ridiculing of the criminals brought three more attempts on his life. These attacks got more deadly with every attempt. Mike was hit in the legs with buckshot and spent several hours in the emergency room getting the pellets removed. The second attempt was much more serious. Someone had fired two shots from a window directly across the street from Mike's office. One of the lead pellets struck him in the chest but did not penetrate the Kevlar vest worn under his suit coat. He was hospitalized for two days for observation.

A stolen car was driven directly into the driver's door of Mike's county-owned car, breaking his left leg, cracking three ribs. He suffered a severe concussion and bruising on the entire left side of his body. The driver of the stolen vehicle attempted to flee on foot, but was quickly captured and held for the police by witnesses to the blatant attempt. Only quick police intervention prevented the perp from being severely beaten.

Salvatori Romanotti was one of three civilians who had been indicted with the others. Mike cut him a deal in return for his testimony against the rest of the defendants. Sal knew he would be killed if anyone found out he was talking, but the prospect of doing serious jail time filled him with terror. The FBI agreed to put Sal in the Witness Protection Program in return for his testimony on RICO charges on the others. Sal prayed he would still be alive for the trials.

Mike stretched his departmental budget way past the breaking point, but he kept Sal from harm for five months. Then three men wearing masks, dressed in police uniforms, broke down the door to the Best Western room where Sal and two plainclothes detectives were holed up. They kidnapped Sal. The detectives were bound, gagged, and locked in the bathroom.

Salvatori Romanotti should have been dead. Two young kids fishing in Wills Creek had found him and called the police. His hands were tied behind his back and he had been shot twice. He was still alive, just barely. For the first time in all his 48 years, Sal was glad to

94   THE WILLS CREEK CHRONICLES

see the cops.

For two weeks, he was in the intensive care unit at Southeastern Medical Center, a hand-picked team of uniformed officers stationed outside his door. The officers were to admit no one without Mike Regan's personal approval. No exceptions!

When Sal was released from the hospital, Regan smuggled him out wearing a police uniform, pretending to be one of the guards going off duty. Sal rode in a black and white to the station house. He changed clothes and was taken out of the station house in the cuffs and leg irons of a felon on his way to the state pen. There was a slight delay in traffic and Sal was once again stashed in a secret hotel room.

When Mike called witnesses in the biggest criminal trial the city had ever seen, the courtroom was packed to the rafters with reporters. He built his case slowly and surely, letting the tension build a little more each day. On the night before Sal was scheduled to testify, Mike offered each of the defendants an opportunity to plead guilty and receive a lighter sentence. In return they would be required to testify against other defendants at future trials. In every case the defendants accepted Regan's offer.

Mike held an impromptu news conference on the courthouse steps after the presiding judge sentenced the defendants. "There are several things I want to say to the public. First, this is only the tip of the iceberg. There are dozens of warrants on my desk waiting to be served. I promised the voters sweeping reforms and I have every intention of keeping that promise.

"I also wish to announce that Salvatori Romanotti died from his wounds three days after he was shot and left for dead in the city dump last year. The man we have been pretending to guard is actually an undercover police officer. This dedicated officer will receive several commendations for service above and beyond the call of duty. There is nothing I can do to ease the pain and suffering for Sal Romanotti's family, except to say I'm sorry for their loss."

He continued, "Early this morning sheriff's deputies and city police officers conducted a series of pre-dawn raids on residences in the county. Twenty-two individuals were arrested and will be charged with various criminal activities and will face a jury of their peers in a courtroom soon."

One jaded news reporter turned to his camera man and said, "Fifty to one says Mike won't be alive in three months."

"You aren't going to find any takers on that sucker bet," said the cameraman, "I doubt if he'll make it a week."

The local newspaper headlines three weeks later read "Car Bomb Blast Kills Mike Regan."

An old man stood in front of the news kiosk reading the headlines. With a snort, he walked on down the street. "It would be just like that damn fool Mike to fake his own death, just so he could grab another bunch of crooks."

This story repeated itself all over town until no one knew for sure if Mike Regan was actually dead or just faking to lull the criminal element into relaxing. To this very day all along Wills Creek, there are old-timers on both sides of the law, who don't believe Mike Regan is really dead. His legend lives on.

LINDA BURRIS

HERMIT OF WILLS CREEK
Sam And The Boys Fix The Cabin's Hole In The Roof

Vietnam War veteran, Sam Tucker, lived in an old log cabin in the woods along Wills Creek. After the war he couldn't do much work around town because of his mental condition. Townspeople were leery of him, his German Shepherd, Butch, had matted fur and a menacing growl.

Sam had long, unkempt, stringy black hair over a ruddy, bearded face. He wore a camouflage shirt and pants full of holes. His combat boots were held together with duct tape.

His home was barely standing. There was a large hole in the roof and several windows looked as if they had been used for target practice. In the front yard was a broken-down pickup truck which he had used to haul firewood for the residents of the town of Willow. Most children in town noticed Sam wasn't friendly so they stayed away from him.

Johnny Temple and his friends, Tim and Tommy Mason, decided to watch Sam and Butch to learn more about their strangeness. Approaching the log cabin, they heard a gunshot. Sam was shooting a rifle at tin cans on a wooden fence. Butch was lying near Sam with his paws covering his ears because of the loud noise.

Sam saw the boys hiding behind some trees and shouted at them to "leave or else!" They were too frightened to run. Johnny started to cry while Tommy and Tim remained still, shaking all over. Sam said to the boys, "What are you boys doing out here?"

"We heard the shooting and wanted to see what you were doing.

We were afraid to talk to you," said Johnny.

"I'm sorry to have scared you boys," Sam replied. I shoot rabbits, turkeys, and deer that provide us our food. I use the tin cans for practice."

The boys asked why he and Butch lived in the woods. "Butch and I like the peace and quiet and the beauty of God's creation. We like hunting and fishing and being by ourselves," Sam explained. Butch moved toward Johnny, gave a cautious sniff, then began wagging his tail. Johnny slowly extended his hand and received a wet lick in response. The boys giggled as Sam let out a huge belly laugh.

"Well boys, Butch thinks you're okay. Why don't you come back tomorrow. I'll see if there is anything here you can help me with," Sam said.

The trio said good-bye to Sam and headed home, talking about Sam and his dog.

Early the next day, the boys arrived at Sam's cabin, excited about helping Sam with things he needed done. Sam greeted them, then looked skyward. Dark clouds approached. "I was going to repair that hole in the roof today, but I'm not sure I should try. Looks like a thunderstorm is coming this way," he mused. "Well, hopefully the storm will pass us this morning."

The boys hoped Sam wouldn't change his mind. They wanted to help repair the roof. Sam needed their help, that was for sure. "How can we help?" asked Johnny.

"Bring me a hammer and nails so I can get this tarp fixed over the hole, replied Sam. "You go back to the ground because our weight might cause the roof to collapse." Johnny, Tim, Tommy and Butch watched Sam on the roof. Suddenly, the wind picked up and started blowing the tarp Sam was affixing to the roof. Just as Sam stood up, a big gust of wind knocked him over. He slid downward and landed on the hard ground below.

"Sam, Sam," the boys cried rushing to the spot where Sam laid. "Can you hear us?"

Sam didn't move. His eyes were closed. The boys were in a quandary until Johnny told the twins, "Hurry home and call 9-1-1. We have to help Sam!"

While the twins were gone, Johnny and Butch stayed beside Sam.

Johnny saw an old blanket on the back porch and laid it over Sam. A few minutes later the ambulance arrived about the same time the twins returned breathlessly to the cabin.

Johnny told the ambulance crew what happened. They put Sam on a gurney, a special collar around his neck and a backboard beneath him. They loaded him into the ambulance and sped off, siren going full blast.

Johnny took Butch back to town with him. When he told his mother about Sam, she called the emergency room to check on Sam's condition. They said he would have to stay in the hospital overnight. He was conscious but had suffered a brain concussion. Johnny's mother asked them to tell Sam the boys had brought his dog to her house until he got home.

Early the next day Johnny's mother and the boys went to the hospital and took Sam back to his cabin. He thanked everyone profusely for their help.

On the way home the boys admitted it had been an exciting adventure, but Johnny said, "I hope our next visit with Sam isn't so crazy."

JOETTA VARANASI

TIPPLE OVER THE CREEK
Work At The Company Story Was His Life Until...

Mr. John worked in the company store and enjoyed helping the people in his coal mining town, allowing them to pay installments for what they bought. He lived at home supporting his mother until her death. A tall gray-haired man with a mustache who took his job seriously, and whose signature was a store apron, he displayed a warm personality and gentleness toward others. But it seemed as though he had to force a smile. Smiling did not come easy to him.

"Good Morning, Mr. John," Mary said in a soft, low, voice with a smile. "It's nippy in the rolling hills today." "Good Morning, Mary," answered Mr. John, "Can I help you with something?

Mary and her children had returned to Tippleville after her husband was killed in a mine in the southern part of the state. She was slim, with long brown hair which she occasionally pulled back with a ribbon. Mary dressed conservatively in maxi skirts and plain blouses. This morning she wore a powder blue sweater that complemented her blue eyes and made them sparkle. A pleasant smile was on her face and she enjoyed talking, but since she lost her husband, Mary wasn't talkative anymore, but she still smiled.

Mary nodded, "Yes, I've got a big list. Mother and I are going to be baking." She tried not to stare at his limp as he moved unsteadily across the room.

Mr. John had little feeling in his left leg. He worked outside as a breaker boy, loading coal cars, got crushed between a coal car and the tracks, and his leg was nearly cut off. Coal was sorted and transported

100 THE WILLS CREEK CHRONICLES

across the creek on a tipple when the mine exploded, generating an electrical fire that destroyed the tipple.

Mary was eight years old when the mine blew up. She remembered lying in bed and gripping the bedposts as they shook. Occasionally, she'd have visions of people running across Wills Creek to the opening of the mine in terror, waiting for loved ones to emerge.

A disaster of that multitude rocked the coal mining town forever. Many folks were haunted when they remembered the evening the earth rumbled and shook, killing 100 miners and leaving hundreds of widows and orphaned children.

"Let me see your list," Mr. John said gently. "I'll fill your order in no time." He pulled items off the shelves and began bagging them. "Don't worry about the money. You can take time to pay me." he said, assuring her that she would be able to take home everything on her list. Mary was surprised. She wasn't sure she could charge at the company store since her husband died.

The next day, Sunday church was unusually crowded to hear a guest pastor.

Mr. John and his mother had always sat in the first row, by the choir, but since her death, he sat in the back row. A sad feeling had buried in his soul, but he was able to hide it. He'd spoken to the pastor, but since his mother's death, he was often depressed.

People stood up and sang, "What a Friend We Have in Jesus," but Mr. John remained silent until when someone tapped him on the shoulder, "Hello," Mary whispered. Mr. John nodded and gave her a warm look, wondering why he hadn't seen her in church before. He noticed a teenage boy dressed in black that was about his age when he was in the mining accident. Behind the boy were two little girls wearing white bonnets and long pink dresses.

The family sat in front of him. Mary's mother sang enthusiastically. Mary turned around several times to smile at Mr. John. Each time she turned and smiled at him, he felt a warm feeling. She went through the motions of singing, but she was distracted by him.

After church Mary's mother invited him to Sunday dinner. He accepted and later enjoyed the meal as well as spending the afternoon sitting on their big, beautiful porch overlooking Wills Creek. He looked at family photos, listened to the girls play the piano and chatted with Mary's mother.

Mr. John took to Ian, Mary's teenage son. When he looked at Ian, he saw himself as a teenage boy. He and Ian connected in many ways. Ian talked about his job at the Woolworth store on Saturdays. They played chess, and made plans to go fishing in Wills Creek.

Mary's family was good for Mr. John. He told them how terrible the pain was when his leg got stuck under the coal car. "I thought I'd never forget how it felt. But I don't feel it anymore," he continued. "I looked back at the explosion and felt happy I wasn't in the mine; I felt sad, because my father and other miners were killed."

The crisp Sunday air made for a beautiful day in the rolling hills, much like the day Mary and Mr. John met in the company store last fall. Townspeople gathered at the church, where Mary and Mr. John were to make an announcement. "We want everyone in town to come to our wedding and celebrate our happiness," Mary sang out with a warm loving smile.

Mr. John glanced out of the window, across the creek. Up on the hill, out of commission was the tipple formerly used to sort the coal. He spoke with a tear in his eye. "We have happy memories and sad memories, but sometime we must turn our sad memories into just memories. We have a future and a past in this town.

Some of our mines are still producing coal, and some are just a memory, but if we look, we'll find happiness. Mary and I want to live forever in Tippleville.

The entire congregation leaped to its feet to congratulate them on their marriage plans.

JOY L. WILBERT ERSKINE

Chances
Old Dogs Really Can Learn New Tricks

As a boy, Calvin McGillicuddy spent most of his time alone, wandering the hills behind his home in Guernsey County. He got to know every rock and rill within a 30-mile radius of Cambridge. Now life had thrown him a stone and he was a widower. His wife, Frannie, had died two years ago. It was a loss he knew he'd never overcome. The solitary time in the hills these days helped him cope with his lonesome routine.

Depression and mood swings stalked him every day. A little too much confusion or too many people and Calvin flew off the handle, like a rocket with all the flight protocol already ticked off.

On this particular Friday morning, Calvin awoke early for no apparent reason. With breakfast over and dishes done, he paced the kitchen floor like a caged tiger waiting for the keeper to bring meat. Finally, he called to his dog, "Chances, we gotta get outta here today. Whaddaya say we head for Salt Fork, drop a fishing line, and have us a fine dinner tonight?"

Chances pranced around the kitchen, toenails clicking on the faded tile floor, excited as a biddy hen with a fox in the coop. Calvin grinned at her enthusiasm. "Well, come on then, girl. Let's get our gear and go."

Chances was good company for Calvin. She was a stray when she found him in the hills the afternoon of Frannie's funeral. He was lost in thoughtful mourning when the big rust-colored mutt bounded up like a runaway rickshaw, almost knocking him over in her exuberance.

"Whoa, girl, where'd you come from?" He spent a few minutes petting and talking to her. When he tried to walk away, the dog followed alongside him and they'd been companions ever since.

"What're the chances you'd find me on the very day I lost my Frannie," he often asked her. The dog would just tilt her head, knitting those bushy brows over her bright brown eyes as if to wonder with him. And so her name became "Chances."

Jumping into Calvin's old rust bucket fishing truck, Chances took her accustomed seat riding shotgun. She hung her head out the window in anticipation of the cool ride ahead while Calvin cranked the clunker to reluctant life. Thirty minutes later they were floating in Calvin's ancient rowboat at his favorite fishing hole on the lake. "Those walleye don't know what's coming," he laughed, winking at Chances. The dog was happy to settle in the bow and wait.

It didn't take long. Calvin got a strike and skillfully set the hook. "Whew! This is gonna be a big one, Chances. He's sure puttin' up a fight," he wheezed, reeling the fish closer. Chances seemed to smile. "We'll have us some nice big fillets for supper," huffed Calvin as he netted his catch over the side of the boat.

"Auuugh!" Calvin dropped the fish into a bucket, clutching his chest. Pain radiated in hot perspiring waves to his shoulder and arm. Chances sprang to his side, licking his face. Calvin grimaced as another wave of pain hit him, then slumped slowly over. Chances' comforting licks metamorphosed into Frannie's welcome home kisses. Calvin smiled. His final whispered words were, "Aw, Frannie, you beautiful redhead, I've missed you so."

DONNA J. LAKE SHAFER

JOE AND THE COMPETITION
The Gibson Boys Have Their Eyes On Sarah Marie

Joe Gibson looked around the place. The pretty farm was well tended. It had been in the family for many years, giving food and shelter to generations of Gibsons who had loved the land.

But today, a fine Saturday, Joe's thoughts turned to girls. One girl in particular. Sarah Marie Johnson had been on his mind a lot lately. She was the oldest of five daughters, all of them nice to look at, but Sarah was special. The truth is, Joe was smitten with Sarah. But what with getting crops in, he hadn't had much time for visiting. As he pondered these matters, Preacher, the black tom cat with the white collar entered the barn followed by the mother cat and their latest litter of kittens. Seeing the little family gave Joe pause to examine his own life. He knew he should be taking a wife soon and starting a family. The folks were getting on in years and Dad hadn't been good. Joe and his brother, Andy, would take over the running of the place soon.

Calling to his brother, Joe said, "What say we pay a visit to the Johnson farm and look in on the girls?"

"Sounds good to me," answered Andy. "I could stand to spend some time with Kathy. I've had my eye on her for a spell. When do you want to go?"

"Well, soon as we finish the chores and get cleaned up. If we stay off the road and go by way of Wills Creek it won't take long. I don't want to go by the Beckett place. Those boys are getting nastier by the day and the old man never shuts up....doesn't say anything, just talks and talks."

Repeating local gossip, "I hear Mrs. Beckett has been poorly," Joe said.

"Not much wonder," replied Andy, "what with a house full of boys who're meaner than snakes and a husband who never lets up."

"O.K.," said Joe, "I'll saddle the horses."

Later, the boys were slicked up and ready to head out. Mrs. Gibson stopped the boys. "Here, I just put up some strawberry preserves. How about stopping by the Beckett place and giving these to Mrs. Beckett? I hear she hasn't been well and she'd probably enjoy them."

As they rode off, Joe mumbled, "Dang, we didn't want to see that bunch but I guess there's no getting 'round it."

Even though the plans had changed, it was still a pleasant ride. The rolling hills of Guernsey County were always a pretty sight, even while riding down a dusty road. The land seemed to be swaying in the gentle breezes over fields of ripening corn and oats and cattle grazing in the fields of thick timothy and clover.

Nearing the Beckett farm, Joe and Andy could see some of the family loafing around on the big wrap-a-round porch. "Darn it," said Andy, "there's the lot of them. I hope none of them take a notion to go getting rowdy."

"It'll be O.K.," Joe replied. "just mind your manners and don't let 'em rile you."

Nearing the house, Joe called out to the group. "Hi, folks, how's it going?"

"Fair to middlin'," answered Mr. Beckett, "Just fair to middlin'. And how are you all?"

"We're good. Me and Andy just thought we'd get out and mosey around a bit today. Mom sent along some strawberry preserves for Mrs. Beckett. And how is the misses?"

"A bit better, I think. Doc Jones came by yesterday and left a tonic of some kind. Says she's a bit run down. Just needs rest."

No wonder, mused Joe to himself. Everyone around knew they all used the poor woman like an old plow horse, never lifting a finger to help with the household chores. Just expected her to wait on them hand and foot. Feeling uncomfortable, he said, "I hope she's better soon. Tell her the folks send their best. Guess we best be moving along. Maybe we'll look in on the Johnsons while we're down this

106   THE WILLS CREEK CHRONICLES

way."

Charlie, the biggest and loudest of the bunch fairly jumped out of his chair, hollering and flapping his arms. "Oh, you don't want to go down there! Why, they got some kind of fever. It's running through the whole family. The lot of them are sick. Probably won't get over it for weeks. You best stay away from there 'til they're all well. Guess it's really catchin'. Ain't that right, boys?" Charlies brothers nodded vigorously.

Disappointed, Joe and Andy took their leave, heading home by way of the creek. It was a cooler ride and the horses could use a cold drink.

When they returned home, much earlier than expected, Joe reported the news to the folks. Everyone speculated on the nature of the illness that had hit the Johnson family, hoping it was more annoying than serious. The boys were disheartened, what with concern about the girls and the day being cut short. Farm work was hard and social occasions rare. Passing time with the likes of the Beckett family hardly fit the bill. Mrs. Gibson, seeing her sons plight, suggested they ride into town and get her a sack of sugar. That wasn't how they'd see the evening going but it was better than nothing.

Things were quiet in the village. A few fellows were hanging around outside the general store, swapping stories and passing the time. Andy stopped for a visit but Joe, still downcast over the days events, entered the building. Hearing a familiar voice that made his breath catch, he turned quickly to see Sarah Johnson. With sparking eyes and about the sweetest smile he's ever seen, she called out. "Why Joe Gibson, how nice to see you. How are you?"

Heart pounding wildly, he answered, "Just fine... now," he stammered. "How have you all been?"

"Oh, we've all been good. Busy, of course, but good."

"All of you? No sickness or anything?'

"None at all. We're all great. All the family and the livestock, too," she said, laughing.

Catching his breath and working up his nerve, Joe asked if it would be alright if he came to see her the next day.

"That should be nice. Why don't you come after church and have dinner with us? Bring Andy along. I know someone who would like to see him," said Sarah, slyly.

"Thanks, I'm sure he'd be happy to join me," smiled Joe.

After making his purchases and saying his goodbyes, he left the store. Collecting Andy, they mounted their horses and headed for home. As they rode out of town, Joe said, "Little brother, do I have a surprise for you!"

Filling Andy in on the latest happenings, Joe said, "Tomorrow, we'll travel along the creek. We'll have us a fine day with some fine people. Then coming back we'll go the main road and pay us a visit at the Beckett place. There are a couple things we're going to discuss with that good-for-nothing, lying bunch.. What a dirty trick to keep us away from those girls! I bet they couldn't get near them and were going to try to kill anyone else's chances. You with me?"

With a big grin and a war whoop, his brother answered, "You betcha. Race you home!"

In high spirits and giving their horses a quick kick, the Gibson boys sped along the road, each lost in his thoughts and the romantic possibilities that tomorrow might bring. Yessiree, Sunday looked to be a good day.

And it was. Nice sunny weather, good eats and the company of the two prettiest girls in the county. And next Saturday night the four would attend the barn dance at the Davis place.

Later, riding at a leisurely pace, Joe's thoughts turned to a spot on the farm that would be perfect for a cozy home, a place that would provide shelter and comfort for another generation of Gibsons.

There was no need to stop by the Beckett place. That score had settled itself.

JERRY WOLFROM

Bulldog Cleaned Up the Town
Hell, Fire And Brimstone Flew In All Directions

We recently underwent a change of pastors at our church. We lost a terrific man and we gained a terrific man. So life is good in our house of worship. But the transition process sent my mind galloping back in time to our small town in Guernsey County, Ohio.

Deweyville included about 400 souls coping with the Great Depression. The Rev. Wallace "Bulldog" Winker was a fixture there. Bulldog had been both a professional boxer and wrestler. His cauliflower ears and smashed nose were fearsome to little kids.

While he was only about 5'9, his shoulders were four feet wide. An imposing sight, he was, as he strode the village streets donned in black trousers, black shirt, black coat and a wide-brimmed black hat with a large gold cross on the front, always looking for sin and temptation.

Bulldog's little cinder block church, which he built himself, was on the banks of Wills Creek. But during the summer, he pitched a huge tent in the village park to hold revival meetings. His congregation grew from about 60 to 150. Town doubters called the noisy band of worshipers Bulldog's Holy Rollers.

After several songs and some hell, fire and brimstone preaching from Bulldog, the believers hollered and screamed and rolled, some as far as the parking lot. Bulldog pulled no punches. He fearlessly cast the first stone because he hated sin and temptation of any kind.

From the hay wagon pulpit he clashed with the devil, using techniques he learned in the fight ring. He strangled the devil, threw him over his shoulder, and trampled him into the dust. Satan never had a chance.

Bulldog regularly charged into Bill's Tavern—known for the best pickled tongue sandwiches in the valley-- and preached to the bar flies. You could hear the sermon all over town. Bible in one hand and a strong stick in the other, Bulldog beat the devil into submission twice a week.

Over at the depot, checker players scattered when Bulldog approached. He'd heard that they sometimes bet a nickle on the game and that to him was sin and temptation run wild.

Jack's Gas Station nearly went out of business because Bulldog often stood near the gas pumps to preach on the evils of cigarettes. Roscoe Shively learned never to let Bulldog into his barber shop because he would charge into the back room and rip up all the girlie posters. He was the poor man's link to God.

But it was the sins of the flesh that he hated most. When he heard that several women who stayed at Maude Latham's Boarding House were up to no good, he raced upstairs and tossed all the mattresses and bed clothes out of the windows and set them afire.

And he didn't only tackle big sins. Bulldog loudly proclaimed that movies were sinful, as was lipstick, tight clothing, playing cards and dancing. All music was sinful, he preached, except gospel music. Anyone who fell to those temptations would "split hell wide open," he shouted.

Bulldog never preached before a radio microphone or TV camera, and he never saw a collection plate with more than twenty dollars in it.

Sadly, a lot of people made fun of him and his band of Holy Rollers, but Bulldog gave temptation the hardest licks I ever saw.

BEVERLY J. JUSTICE

Mystery of Sutler's Pond
Boy Solves Decades-Old Mystery

The fishing rod tapped rhythmically against the handlebars as eleven-year-old Bryce Dalton coasted his bicycle down Eighth Street Road. Sutler's pond, ten minutes from Bryce's north side home, had been known for years as having the biggest and tastiest bluegills in the area. However, bringing home a stringer of fish was not on Bryce's mind that day.

Goose bumps peppered his arms, in spite of the 80-degree heat, but Bryce knew he must return to the pond. What he had seen Tuesday afternoon was just as real as the wild roses growing at the side of the road. But he could tell no one. He would pour his energy into solving this event that had plunged itself into his life, but he could not tell anyone.

Last Tuesday began with Bryce helping his brother, Tyler, wash the car. Tyler, who was 17, still gloated about his success on the high school swim team and already was checking colleges with strong swimming programs. Bryce joked to himself that someday Tyler would sprout gills and fins.

At one o'clock Tuesday afternoon, Bryce's best friend, Brian, arrived with a carton of "killer nightcrawlers" for their first day of summer fishing. The boys loaded their bicycles, packed some snacks, then headed for Eighth Street Road.

"Get ready for a Fish Ohio award!" shouted Brian as they turned onto the gravel path leading from Eighth Street Road to Sutler's pond.

After baiting their hooks, the young fishermen settled on the pond's bank, each with a pole in one hand and a bottle of Gatorade in the other. The aroma of honeysuckle and freshly-mowed grass filled the air as the afternoon sun glazed the pond with gold. The first hour produced four bluegills and one small bass, which the boys returned to the pond with instructions to come back next year. After another two hours and only one more bluegill, the two decided to call it a day.

"I saw my dad checking out the bikes at Walmart," Brian said as they gathered their gear. "Bet I get a new one for my birthday next month!"

"That's great, Brian," Bryce replied, strapping his fishing pole to the bicycle. "I told my dad I'd like a new tackle box."

Then Bryce saw it. In the pond, about 25 feet from the bank on which he stood, was a ghost. It was a boy, who looked to be about Tyler's age, with bushy hair and strange clothing. He was wearing a blue and yellow printed shirt cinched by a wide black belt at the ghost's slim hips. He was knee-deep in the water, although Bryce knew that the pond was at least 10 feet deep in that area. The ghost looked directly at Bryce while pointing downward, just to his side.

"You daydreaming, or what?" Brian's voice jolted Bryce back to the world of the living.

"Oh, nothing. Just wondering how many fish are in the pond."
As he mounted his bike, Bryce took another quick glance. The ghost was gone.

I handled that so cool, Bryce thought, following Brian onto Eighth Street Road.

This was not Bryce's first encounter with the supernatural. He had an uncanny rapport with animals, even as a toddler. He also had a knack for finding lost items, such as car keys, books, jewelry, and even his dad's briefcase. However, these could be explained as luck, or perhaps a gift. But ghosts were a whole different ballgame, and most people do not play that game.

When Bryce was four years old, his parents bought him a new "grown-up" bed that he loved. However, Bryce did not understand why an old man in a dark blue suit would sit at the foot of his bed every night. Bryce did what he thought a good boy should do. He asked his parents to tell the man that he may sit on the floor, but please stay off the bed.

112   THE WILLS CREEK CHRONICLES

The memory was bitterly painful: Tyler roared with laughter. Bryce's father shook his head and rolled his eyes; his mother insisted that he must have been dreaming. Bryce never forgot the mysterious man on his bed. He knew he hadn't been dreaming.

When Bryce was seven his father taught him and Tyler how to skip stones in a part of Wills Creek known as the Fishbasket. Bryce thought the name was not fitting, as the only fish he had ever caught there was a scrawny catfish. After finding a flat stone, Bryce heaved it with a snap of his wrist onto the creek's surface. It skipped three times before sinking at the feet of a native American standing on the opposite bank.

"Hey, Dad, look at the Indian!" Bryce shouted before he could think.

Again, he faced laughter and accusations of having watched too many westerns. Bryce swore then that he forever would keep his gift (more aptly, a curse) a secret.

His resolve was tested that autumn after school had begun. In the cafeteria, Abbie Gates was sitting with her friends three tables from Bryce. Abbie's mother was standing behind her, with a hand gently resting upon Abbie's shoulder.

The problem was Mrs. Gates had died from cancer six weeks earlier. Bryce watched as children continued to chat and laugh, and even walked through Mrs. Gates, unaware that she was among them. Bryce handled the situation well, he thought. No one had suspected anything. No laughter, no ridicule. He wondered if he could manage the current situation as well.

He hard-braked his bicycle at the end of the gravel path, causing bits of gravel to fly like frightened birds. After attaching a sinker just above the unbaited hook, he cast into the area where the ghost had been. He was reeling back when he hit a snag. After a series of tug-and-release, the 10-pound test fishing line broke. Whatever was out there was big and heavy.

Bryce retrieved the phone from his pocket and called Tyler.

"Tyler, do me a huge favor, please! Bring your diving gear to the pond. There's something big in there!"

"Bryce, are you nuts? You know that old man Sutler doesn't allow swimming."

"He's still out of town. I'm not kidding, Tyler. Something is out there. Remember a couple years ago when someone stole the safe from Connor's store? They've never found it. Maybe it's here."

"Okay, I'll do it, but you owe me one."

When Tyler arrived, Bryce pointed to the spot.

"It's about 25 feet straight out."

"There had better be something there," Tyler grumbled, putting on his fins and goggles.

After Tyler submerges, Bryce counted the seconds on his wristwatch. "Come on," he muttered.

Twelve seconds later, Tyler burst through the pond's surface, frantically pulling off his goggles.

"There's a car down here!"

The next couple hours were a blur. Professional divers, sheriff's deputies, tow trucks, the coroner, and even a television crew lined the banks of Sutler's pond. Most of the pond was now surrounded by yellow tape.

Tyler, who had been using the phone almost nonstop since the discovery, put the phone into his pocket and told Bryce that their mother wanted them to come home. The boys loaded Bryce's bicycle into the trucnk. Bryce was glad for the comfort of an air-conditioned car after this exhausting day.

"Mom said they had a newsbreak on TV about it already," said Tyler. "They think the guy is a teenager who was reported missing back in 1971. He simply disappeared without a trace."

"Wow, 1971," Bryce marveled. "That explains his wild hair and weird clothes."

Oops!

Tyler's eyes got so big that Bryce was afraid they would fall from their sockets,

"How do you know what he looked like?" Tyler's voice tone was one of shock, confusion, and a touch of fear.

"You knew that kid was in the pond the whole time, didn't you? What's going on, Bryce?"

Bryce sighed deeply, wiped his forehead, then began:

"Tyler, do you remember when I was four years old and Mom and Dad bought me a new bed . . ."

BARBARA KERNODLE-ALLEN

Hunting Firsts
Jim Found More Than He Expected

Hunting alone for the first time, 13 year old Jim proudly shouldered Pa's gun. He missed the companionship and support of his father and uncle, but the men, as well as most folks in Cambridge, this day in 1918, were "laid up with the grippe." It was the epidemic known as the "Spanish Flu." Factories shut down. Whole families took sick and died. Streets deserted, folks were afraid to be near anyone who might be ill.

Proud and excited to be trusted to provide meat for the family, Jim made his way across a shallow place in Wills Creek crossing into "hunting meadows," one of the best places to "bag game" in the county. Animals of all kinds crossed the meadow to drink from the creek. There were ' possums, coons, rabbits, ground hogs and plenty of deer to be had. Jim wanted to kill enough so Ma could feed their family and leave a basket of food on the doorstep of the sick neighbors next door.

With a bag full of squirrel, rabbit and ground hog, Jim took a bead on a big buck. Just as he squeezed off a shot, another shot rang out. As the deer crumpled, the most beautiful girl he'd ever seen stepped out of the shadowy thicket. Waist length red-gold curls glistened in the waning light. A vision in gingham. Sobbing, she dropped her pistol. "Oh! I killed him. The poor thing! I'm sorry...so sorry but, we gotta eat."

Jim stared open-mouthed. He knew it was his shot that took the buck, but breathless, he was spellbound by the scene unfolding before him. Feeling hot… cold… shaky…wanting to cry, too. Trying to clear his throat he coughed. It was more like a wheeze.

Huge, tear filled blue eyes, settled on the mesmerized boy. "Oh, please. Help me. I can't lift it." Thinking to lay his rightful claim on the deer, Jim dropped to one knee, whipped out his knife, and began field dressing his prize. "Darn! How could she think she'd taken the deer with that little pistol?"

She knelt to help, and a lock of hair brushed the back of his bloody hand, sending shivers up his arm. "I ain't never hunted before. My folks took sick and the little ones are hungry. There warn't no choice," she said.

Looking into the delicate, faintly freckled, tear- stained features, Jim sighed. How could he tell her the buck was his kill? "I'll carry it for yuh. Where do yuh live? Maybe next time you kin get somthin' a little smaller."

Returning home with the bag full of small game that night, Jim didn't tell Ma he'd bagged his first deer, that he'd carried it half a mile up the ridge and given it away, or that he'd promised to teach a girl to hunt. He went to bed with a smile, dreaming of the deer he'd shot and the "dear" he'd like to catch.

PAM RITCHEY

Dust and Dreams
Don't Fall Asleep In This House

"It was just another dream," Della thought as her body jerked awake. She had been running through the woods with her children, trying to reach their hidden refuge before the Indians caught them.

Della lived a solitary life in the cabin which had been in the Hostutler family since they settled near Wills Creek in 1754. Her name even came from her great-great-grandmother who helped build the cabin. The present-day Della had painstakingly restored it to its original condition only adding modern conveniences which she craftily concealed to blend with the décor.

"I'd better rouse Raymer. I can't believe he's still abed", she thought to herself as she headed toward their feather-tick under the eaves. "What am I doing? I must still be caught up in those crazy dreams. Wake up Della. It's the twenty-first century, not the eighteenth!"

She shook her head, trying to get a grip on reality as she realized there was no feather-tick. The old oak secretary which occupied the space under the eaves hid her laptop computer.

I feel like I've been asleep for ages, Della thought as she opened her computer. The keys began to chatter as she typed in notes on her latest dream. Okay, let's see… I can remember the Thompson's settling on the next farm over, the Beattys and Gombers arriving and plotting out the town.

Her older notes covered coming out on the banks of a gorgeous creek and Raymer naming it Will's Creek after her daddy and saying they had reached their new home site. She read of giving birth to

Esther and teaching her to read then Oscar, William, Jennie Maple and Paul. She had a vivid memory of these things happening. This is crazy, how can I be living my ancestor's life through dreams. How is this possible?

Della's world became filled with confusion. Her dreams of living her great-great-grandmother's life was entwined with the reality of present day to the point of her not knowing which was the dream. She seemed to be aging along with the woman in her dreams, so she reasoned the woman in 2009 had to be the dream. Eventually, life in 2009 became a distant memory; her dreams of it came less and less frequently as she lived out her life surrounded by her family.

"Della hasn't been in to pick up her heart medication for two months now. She always calls in her refills like clockwork. Thanks so much for coming out with me to check on her," said Diane, owner of Westside Pharmacy.

"She probably just switched drug stores and didn't tell you," Deputy Harris said as he knocked on the cabin door.

"Deputy Harris, come quick!" said Diane as she peered in the window off the front porch.

"Someone's in the bed. She looks dead! It can't be Della, this woman's too old."

DNA testing confirmed that the old woman in the bed was in fact 28-year-old Della Hope Hostutler. Listed on the death certificate is "Death due to natural causes of aging."

JERRY WOLFROM

Kissing in the Moonlight
Ida Mae Dill Was A Special Gal

Planners for our class reunion called and asked if I'd prepare a funny speech, tied in some way to those great days at tiny Wills Creek High. Immediately my first flame came to mind, Ida Mae Dill, the girl who taught me how to kiss those many years ago.

Ah, the innocence of those days of long ago. Ida Mae was two years older and four inches taller than me.

Researching kissing seemed like a good idea and would give the speech a great opening. Who invented kissing, I wondered.

One theory is that cave men got the idea after watching lizards slobbering all over each other. When they tried it on their wives, both parties liked it, and the rest is history. Let me say that Ida Mae could have taught those naked, bearded cave guys a thing or two.

At our school, the senior prom, as in most schools, was a special event. A few showoffs danced to records, but most of us just sat there and watched. As the evening wore on, Ida May suggested we go out to Necker's Nob, a grassy knoll above Wills Creek, said to be popular with teenage couples looking for some privacy. Ida Mae said it was a great place to gaze at the full moon.

There were only two other cars there and the view of the moon was beautifully romantic. At least until the car windows steamed up. In those days the older students talked about "technique," but none of us farm boys had any idea about technique. But Ida May did. And how!

Kissing, I learned later, "happens when tumescense occurs in the human body, causing rhymethic contractions of various muscles and glands." Trust me, Ida May had the latter.

Most innocent kids in those days believed in a theory that said there can be no real kissing if the girl is taller than the boy. But Ida Mae and I learned quickly that if she took off her high heels and I stood on a small rock, things went swimmingly.

Later that night she confessed that her ambition was to get married right after graduation and she had several prospects in mind, including me.

The Wills Creek Class of '48 got their diplomas two weeks later and scattered to various parts of the country. I didn't see Ida May again, but heard years later she had outlived three husbands – a rich Washington banker, a struggling crabber in Maryland and a daredevil rodeo clown in Oklahoma.

A week before our reunion she called me to catch up and chatter about the upcoming class reunion. I told her my speech was a funny look back at our prom date.

After giggling, she said, "Look, you're single and I'm single. So how about the two of us going to the reunion together? For old times' sake. Is Necker's Nob still there?"

"Oh, yes, and just as popular as ever."

After our conversation I hurriedly checked the calendar. Sure enough there would be a full moon on the evening of the reunion.

There's no dramatic way to end this story except to say that our visit to Necker's Nob was even more exciting than it was 50 years ago.

J. PAULETTE FORSHEY

THE ESTATE OF
THADDEUS P. LAMBERT
A Bid For A Rare Book Library Brings A Different Type Of Wealth

Cuilean Keeley caressed the books leathery spines with his fingers and felt a curious tingling course through the tips, much as one would feel if one had just grabbed a live electrical wire. When he had begun his search some ten years back, their trail was already fifty years old. Researching material for his masters' degree in archeology, he had come across vague notations scrawled in the margins of an old, forgotten text, which first gave him hope to their existence. From that tiny morsel of information, gleaned so many years before, he'd scoured university and historical archives, old letters, and shipping manifestos for any further hint of their whereabouts. Discovered quite by accident, wedged between a ledger's pages, a faded Daily Jeffersonian newspaper clipping, concerning an unidentified missing girl, and her unbalanced employer, a Mr. Thaddeus P. Lambert, in Cambridge, Ohio. Next, he had located a delinquent tax notice that led him to an old obituary and finally to the announcement of an estate auction being held this very weekend.

He'd traveled far to attend this auction, selling all, save for the clothes on his back, to make the trip. Wearing a much worn jean-jacket, a faded blue work shirt, tattered jeans, and thin-soled tennis shoes, he walked up the weathered, graying flagstone path of Lambert's estate. He could hear the soft babbling brook, an offshoot of the mighty Wills Creek behind the house. Cuilean's clear, olive skin, abundant black hair, thick black lashes, and deep green eyes caught the attention of

THE ESTATE OF THADDEUS P. LAMBERT **121**

many gathered at the auction. When he was a child, his grandmother, fair-haired and pale-skinned, had once told him he was a throwback to their Celtic heritage; a Black Celt is what she called him.

Cuilean paused on the flagstones. Seeing the shutters closed, half-closed or hanging askew, reminded him of the flirting winks of dirty old men to pubescent girls. Now, after all these years, the house with its lumbering behemoth shape rose fat like a well-fed slug to sit beneath a labyrinth of vegetation. Curious, the paint should have peeled and flaked along the house's sides and around its exotic, carved trimmings, but only for a slight yellowing to tell of age, the facade stayed whole. He listened as the gossips twittered that once the long, wide, graceful, wrap-around porch sported delicate white wicker furniture. Alas, only crumbling remains, memories of the past, lay resting on floorboards that protested loudly as the inquisitive bidders trod upon them, allowing a musty earth smell to seep through the boards. In particular, Cuilean noted, the odor of a wet, wind-swept, dark, cold, forgotten graveyard hung like Spanish moss on the railings and doorways.

Cuilean marveled as he heard the estate, its contents, and last-known two occupants still being talked about in hushed whispers after all these years. The owner, a quiet English scholar of means in his late fifties — a one Thaddeus P. Lambert, so the gossips narrated — had done away with his beautiful, mysterious, and very young female assistant. Where she had come from, or how she had gotten there, no one could say. As the story went, the gossips whispered, most remembered her steadily walking as though on an already fixed path to Mr. Lambert's front door. She had carried a faded old carpetbag, a suitcase of sorts from yesteryear. Her dress, once brightly colored, had been a pale ghost of itself, clinging to her womanly figure, as her stockinged legs had swished rhythmically with each determined stride. Her face they never saw, for she had worn a large-brimmed hat over long, tousled auburn tresses.

The gossips whispered that Thaddeus had never stood trial. No crime could be proven, though the girl was missing. They'd never found her body or any hint of foul play. Only the ravings of Lambert's that *they* had taken her, and never saying who *they* were, was what condemned him to a sterile, white, padded room. As to why Thaddeus

122 THE WILLS CREEK CHRONICLES

supposedly had done what he had, that was left up to many for speculation.

Some said he did it in a fit of jealous rage, whether over a mysterious lover or professional rivalry, the distinction was never made clear. Others claimed he'd always been an odd duck, too bookish, a bit queer in the head with his lofty notions. They knew all along from the way he coveted his extensive library of rare books, like so many precious gems, it was only a matter of time before he went completely over that proverbial mental ledge.

Listening to the gossips, hearing these descriptions of old Lambert, he snorted in knowing self-recognition. Being a scholar himself, he admitted burrowing into the studies of ancient, lost, and forgotten peoples, becoming heedless at times to those around him. Rubbing his fingertips together, he could still feel a residue of the tingle.

The bidding had been high, yet he had known no matter what the cost, he must own these books...and now they were his. Reverently he opened one. A soft, sweet floral aroma tickled his nostrils. His nose twitched at the sweet smell as a lazy grin spread across his face, and one eyebrow raised, displaying his surprise and delight at finding it there. This was the scent that invaded and perfumed his nightly dreams. Her fragrance, sent to him by them. Hugging the book to his chest like a lover, he shut his eyes as her ethereal form teasingly swam before his closed lids. She wore in his dreams the same brightly colored dress faded to a pale ghost of itself. Her hair, a mass of auburn, copper, cinnamon, and gold, tantalizingly obscured her face. He knew to see her face, to touch her supple, satiny skin, to feel her move beneath him, he would have to find a way to slip between their once-creamy sheets, now yellowed and edges brown-tinged. Pulling himself from his daydreams, glancing about, he noticed the odd stares and muted whispers from those still there to buy and those who had come to simply ogle.

He respectfully packed the books into a faded old carpetbag. He'd bid on the thing and won it with his last dollar. The books packed safely away, he found the feel of the carpetbag's handle comforting in his hand. He slipped unobserved behind the house, down a weed-choked path to await the departure of his fellow bidders and the arrival of nightfall.

The old basement window gave easily under the pressure of his foot. He wiggled his lanky six-foot-plus frame through the opening to drop soundlessly to the earthen floor below. Never having been to the house, he knew its floor plan. Carefully, he reached up to retrieve the carpetbag, drawing it through the opening to hug it close to his chest. Extracting a small flashlight from his jean-jacket's inner pocket, he turned it on, gathering his bearings. To his left were the stairs leading upward. Taking them one at a time, stepping, waiting, stepping, waiting, making sure each one would support his weight, he made his way slowly to the top. At their summit, he gently pushed on the door facing him. It gave in a rush, sending him sprawling across the kitchen floor. He lay there momentarily stunned, the wind knocked out of him. Picking up the flashlight and the bag he gingerly made his way to the library. A full moon shone through the now-drapeless windows illuminating the rooms. Cuilean stepped into the library. The floor to ceiling shelves that lined the walls, once filled to their capacity, now gaped open like so many empty, hungry maws. He stepped into the middle of the room, sat down cross-legged, took one book out, and began to read.

Night turned into day and day into night several times over and still he read. His hair, once shiny, black and neatly trimmed, turned dull, unruly and long. His eyes became flat and red-rimmed. He did not eat or drink as normal men during this time: he had no need. The books nourished his earth-bound form, and as he learned their words, their secrets unfolded bit by bit unto him. To his dismay, she coyly kept her distance.

Frustrated, he stood up and at first paced the library to and fro. Next, he wandered from room to room re-reading, re-reciting their words over and over. The dust and dirt on projections, shelves, and counter tops that he passed receded, leaving bright, polished wood in his wake. Like a great creeping thing, their magic seeped through him, rolled from him in enormous waves. Windows sparkled in the first morning light. Inside and out sagging wood straightened as if new, shutters righted themselves, and encroaching vegetation retreated.

And the towns' people began to notice and whisper among themselves.

Deep between their covers, they rejoiced. After a millennium and a century by half, they had found an equal worthy of their most prized possession. Unlike that one Thaddeus P. Lambert, every test, every task they asked of this new man, he passed. Yet, she kept her distance. They were perplexed. They coaxed, they pleaded. He was the ying to her yang, they whispered. Finally, in desperation, when they were about to abandon all hope, one voice slipped silently up to her asking, "Why?"

"Love!" she cried. "Love! All does not matter save for genuine love. Does his heart love? Would it, could it, love me?" She entreated in anguish.

"Love?" They had welcomed her into their world, found her worthy of their knowledge and she lamented for an emotion? They retreated into themselves, searching their collective minds, posing the questions to all. Day turned into night three times over as they pondered. All were to agree. Yes, she was correct; without love, knowledge was only a tear in a vast ocean. They went to him, finding Cuilean sitting against a wall. Settling over him like an early morning fog, they lulled him into to a deep slumber.

Cuilean dreamed she came to him. She stood one tall man's-length from him and yet, she hesitated. She began to reach out her hand to him and stopped. He frowned, then seeing her tremble, he at last understood. Smiling, he opened his arms wide and called to her with the song his soul sang only for her. She ran to him and he crushed her to him. He brushed the curls from her face and saw the beauty that lay hidden there. Cupping her face between his hands, he rained kisses upon her forehead, eyelids, cheeks, and settled on her mouth, tasting its sweetness. She whispered her name to him, and his smile widened. He lowered her down, removing their clothing, he covered her and warmed her with his body, and they loved.

Outside, the townspeople had gathered. "Not again," they cried, "not again in our town!"

Inside, they loved...and the ancient books, *their* words, *their* beliefs, became a tiny spark that glowed a fiery red.

Outside, the crowd grew and they began to travel up the flagstone path of the estate of Thaddeus P. Lambert.

The ground and the house began to tremble, shake, and swell. Vines stretched forward to tangle and choke the flagstone path. Slate crashed from the roof. Shutters slammed shut or fell from their hinges. Windows exploded thousands of shards of brilliance into the crowd, sending them running. A low moan, concentrated and pain-filled permeated the air as walls fissured and split...and the house began to succumb. Those that were there later swore they heard a woman's effort-filled cry of joy and a man's triumphant roar of pride emanate from the house's interior as they watched the house fold into itself.

And as the dust settled, much to the amazement of all, a fiery-headed babe crawled naked from the rubble chortling gleefully.

They rejoiced.

DICK METHENY

SERIAL KILLER ON THE LOOSE
Jealousy Motivates The Social Security Serial Killer

Detective-Sergeant Roland Winston, at seven in the morning, was already on his way downtown, when he got the call on his handheld radio. Damn! Another homicide! An elderly lady returning home from the movies with her neighbor had most likely surprised a burglar. Her body was discovered early this morning by her nephew, Edward Brooks, and his girlfriend, Sybil Tannenbaum. He slapped his hand against the steering wheel, cursing under his breath. This made the third homicide in six days. This town averaged only twelve to fifteen homicides a year, not anywhere near three in one week. Winston called dispatch to ask them to call one of his two detectives, Don Wilson at home and send him to the crime scene.

Normally, Don Wilson worked the afternoon shift, but he had doubled over onto the night shift and only gotten off duty an hour ago. Winston hated to call Wilson away from his sleep, but his only other detective, Jill Wakeman, had to be in court this morning.

Due to budget constraints, the police department was badly understaffed. Winston supervised homicide, robbery, and drug enforcement. This morning he was on his way to meet with a SWAT team leader to coordinate a raid on drug dealer. After that he'd have to talk with the robbery squad to talk about a rash of liquor store robberies. Hopefully he would get time to deal with the murder case before lunch.

Later that day, Winston and Don Wilson were eating lunch in Winston's office. Wilson took another bite of his monster burger, washed it down with black coffee and said, "At first glance, it looked like a B&E gone bad, but there are too many little details that don't add up. Ed Brooks is her only living relative and he has an alibi. The victim, Sarah Dillworth, was a frail, older woman. She would have been easy to overpower and tie up. There was no need to kill her. The B&E was a halfway attempt. Some drawers were tossed, the mattress and pillows were torn apart, but the couch cushions, kitchen and bathroom cabinets weren't touched."

Winston nodded and asked, "Cause of death?"

"My money is on a blow to the head with a blunt instrument. Of course, that's just my guess, pending the autopsy report."

"Did the door-to-door canvas turn up anything?"

"Yeah. There were several irate citizens who weren't too happy about being harassed by the police at that hour of the morning. The ones that weren't mad about being dragged out of bed were mad because the police weren't doing enough to protect them."

"That is just human nature."

"One of Mrs. Dillworth's neighbors told us she'd been going out with a Jonathan Harper for several months."

Winston quipped, "Well, all the detective novels I read say the motive is most often love or money. Odds are we need to track the money. Crimes of passion aren't usually found among the Geritol set."

Wilson agreed, "Well, I'll track the money angle first. We won't get any reports from the crime scene crew or the coroner until at least tomorrow."

"Jill should be out of court by now. I'll meet with the two of you at five this afternoon and we'll look at these cases again."

They got together in Winston's office just after five. Jill Wakeman, arrived looking like a million dollars, dressed in a black pants suit and gray silk blouse. She was still on the sunny side of forty. She had earned her detective shield the hard way, ten years on uniformed patrol, most of it on the midnight shift.

Wilson wandered in, looking exactly like what he was, a worn-out grouchy old flatfoot with the coffee jitters, wearing a badly rumpled navy blazer and tan slacks. He was a charter member of the over-the-hill gang; over fifty, overweight, over his head in debt and seriously overtired. He had been a detective for 15 years and during that time, he had turned down at least two offers to move up the chain of command. He had forgotten more about police work than most officers ever learned.

Winston closed the door, opened both windows, took an ashtray from his middle desk drawer, and placed it on his desk. "The smoking lamp is lit. Don, what have you got on this latest murder?"

"The coroner estimated the time of death at eleven p.m., although it could be an hour one way or the other. I went over the reports, interviewed Brooks and his girlfriend and double-checked their alibi. They were with two other couples at a night club across town until two a.m. The money trail is a dead end. She didn't have enough in the bank to bury her."

"Jill?"

"I reviewed the other two murders and came up with zilch. They are very similar to Don's case. Wanda Dockett, a widow, age 70, was the first victim. She went to dinner and a concert with a friend on Friday night. The friend dropped her off at home at eleven p.m. and she was dead an hour later. Victim Number Two Myra Vincent, another widow, age 64, went to the movies on Sunday night with a friend. She came home around eleven and was dead less than two hours later. In both cases, the cause of death was a blow to the head with a blunt instrument."

"Did you interview the friend in either of these cases?"

"No. We could not locate victim number one's friend. But a canvas of the neighborhood found a neighbor lady that told them Mrs. Dockett had been going out with this friend for a few months. Her description was pretty vague. Victim number two's neighbor gave us a name and description of Mrs. Vincent's friend. His name is John Harrison, approximately 5' 10", late sixties, white hair and a dark tan."

Winston said, "Well, that tears it, victim number three, Sarah Dillworth is a widow, age 72. She also went to dinner and local comedy club with a friend."

Winston stubbed out his cigarette and said, "There is way too much coincidence involved for these cases not to be tied together. I want John Harrison and Jonathan Harper picked up and brought in for questioning."

Wakeman exhaled a cloud of smoke, "Damn! We're about dense. John Harrison and Jonathan Harper, I bet they're one and the same."

Wilson slapped his palm on the desk, "I should be boiled in oil! I never made the connection. Beauty and brains in a cop is unusual, Ms. Wakeman, and you just happen to have both."

Winston grabbed a phone and dialed the three-digit desk sergeant's number, "Sergeant, this is Rollie Winston. I want a team of uniforms rolling right now. Wilson will be right out with the address. No, I don't give a damn if there isn't anyone available. You make it your job to get someone available, right now! If you don't have a team rolling in five minutes, you will be walking a beat on the south end of Wills Creek until you retire. Am I making my self clear? Good."

He turned to Wilson. "You give the desk sergeant the address, then you are off duty until noon tomorrow. You're dead on your feet. Take a cab if you don't think you can drive. Don't even try to argue, go."

"Wakeman, you scare up someone from the prosecutor's office and get them down here ASAP. We don't want to screw up on this one."

Less than one hour later, a James Hamer, alias Jonathan Harper and John Harrison, was taken into police custody. In the apartment listed to John Harrison, uniformed officers found two cell phones. Crime scene investigators quickly linked one of the phones to all of the victims. On this phone were several pictures of each of the victims with John Hamer.

Armed with enlarged copies of the pictures, Winston and Jill Wakeman began their preliminary interview. Shamefully, he confessed to living a double life. Hamer admitted he had been dating the three women, but he vehemently denied killing any of them. He lived with his wife, Betty, clear across town from the victims.

"My wife is a dominating bitch, to put it mildly. We have been married for 27 years and she has always been abusive. Betty physically attacks me, beating and kicking for little or no reason. I created John Harrison and Jonathan Harper so I could socialize with other people without my wife finding out about it. But I would never hurt anyone. I enjoyed going out with those ladies. They treated me like I was a real person, not like my wife treats me."

"When I read in the newspaper about Wanda being killed, I was devastated. Then I saw where Myra had been murdered, I got scared. This morning when I heard about Sarah, I was terrified. Someone is murdering those women because they were going out with me. That someone could only be my wife, Betty."

Winston looked at Jill. She nodded. He picked up the phone and said, "Sergeant, send two units to pick up Mrs. Betty Hamer. Consider her armed and dangerous."

JOY L. WILBERT ERSKINE

Familiar Trappings
An Aged Woman Awaits Her Time

Mildred Patterson carefully held her apron flat against her stomach as she pushed another log into the flames. "I never fancied dying in a fire," she mumbled crossly. "There's surely a better way to go. I don't want them to find me in the ashes next spring."

Leaning back into her ancient wooden rocker, she scanned the dark room around her. Her eyes were still as clear as the day she was born, 93 years ago, in 1916. The only light she needed came from the fire in the hearth. She'd extinguished the wick in her great-grandmother's oil lamp. Now she sat in the fire's glow, remembering.

The familiar trappings of her family's lives comforted her tonight. They'd lived quietly, almost invisibly, along Wills Creek since 1785. The forested hills of her great-great-grandfather's Ohio military land grant had been home to four generations of Patterson's. Above the fireplace hung his muzzleloader, dusty now, its pitted bayonet stalwart and ready, as the man himself had always been.

On the south wall under the window stood Mother's treadle sewing machine, a gift from Father when Mildred was a young girl. The oak cabinet carried the patina of years of loving use. Mildred still sewed her own dresses and aprons on it. The sturdy little rocker she sat in had been built and carved by her great-grandfather when he was a young man.

George, her husband, smiled down at her from a silver-framed portrait on the mantel. He'd been gone for seven years now. All around her family history beckoned, each cherished memento with its own story to tell of family members long lost and dearly missed.

Clasping her hands and closing her eyes, Mildred offered a prayerful plea. "Oh, when will it be my turn, Lord? When will I see them all again? There's no purpose left for me in this world. I'm just waiting for my life to end. Why am I still here—an old woman, alone in the hills? Please, won't you come for me soon? I've done all I know how to do. I'm tired and ready to come home."

An icy December blast rattled the front porch screen, startling Mildred from her fervent petitions. "Who's there?" she cried without thinking, then realized she hadn't slipped the hook and eye closed. "Drat! That wind will rip the door off'n the hinges, sure as the dickens, if I don't go out there and shut it proper." Stiff with age, she hoisted her old body up, wrapped a shawl around her thin shoulders, and braced for the cold.

Opening the door just enough, she stepped onto the porch. Her arthritic fingers fumbled with the screen door hook until she had it safely latched. Her breath hung like an icy fog around her. "It's colder'n a witch's tit out here," she exclaimed to herself, shivering.

From the far end of the porch, a quiet moan reached her ears and her heart jumped. Slowly, fearfully, she turned toward the voice, her breath choked up inside her. It was a child, eight or nine years old, sleeping with Mildred's cat on a ragged stuffed chair, a frozen old quilt their only covering. "Oh my word, child! What are you doing out here in the hills in this weather?" Stepping carefully forward, Mildred called, "Wake up, wee one. Are you all right? Wake up."

There was no answer. Fear gripped her heart and squeezed hard. With the forgotten strength of earlier years, she gathered the boy into her arms. There seemed to be nothing to him, he felt so light. "Oh, I hope he'll be all right," she fretted, her voice choking. She carried him swiftly into the warmth of the house.

"You're frozen half to death, child. Wake up, wake up!" Tears streamed down her wrinkled cheeks as she laid him on the sofa near the hearth. She massaged his little face and body like one would rub a near-stillborn pup, with an energy she'd not had in years. "Come on, child! Don't give up now!"

A low moan escaped the boy's lips. Mildred sank to the floor beside him, pulling him into her lap. She wrapped her shawl snugly around him, rocking and peering through tears into his face, searching for any sign of awakening. "Are you in there, child? It's going to be all right, just wake up now and it'll be all right," she sobbed. "Don't die. Dear God, please don't let him die," she whispered. "It appears you're not quite finished with me yet, and I suppose I can accept that. You'll have to help me though. Just point me a'right, that'll be good enough."

For fifteen long minutes, Mildred rocked and prayed. At last, the boy's eyes fluttered open. Mildred gasped in tearful joy. She hugged him close and looked heavenward through shining eyes. "Thank you, God, for answering prayers for me, and for this young'un too. We needed you tonight and here you are, just like always. I should'a knowed it. I won't be forgettin' again. I'll just leave things in your hands."

DONNA J. LAKE SHAFER

AN OFFER WE REFUSED
Now We Know How Gen. Custer Felt

We had just about had it! Though B.J. and I enjoyed our husbands and children, we needed a break from camping. Let's face it, bobbing around in a fishing boat on an isolated lake in Quebec for days on end was just not our idea of a vacation. It had become a yearly practice and it was beginning to wear a bit thin.

We were doing the same things that we did at home without any of the conveniences. Cooking on camp stoves, no washers or dryers. Nope, laundry was done off shore with wet clothes spread over bushes to dry. A bath was a bar of soap, a wash cloth and a dip in the lake while wearing bathing suits, for gosh sake. And bathroom facilities? Ha! A walk to the woods, a roll of toilet tissue in hand and a companion to watch out for Indians, bears, and poison ivy. I'm talking primitive camping. And I'm not kidding about bears and Indians.

So, B.J. and I made our declaration of independence. Today, the guys and kids would fish and we would not. We'd pack them shore lunches and they could fish all day, but we were staying in camp.

"But what if someone comes around, the Indians or God-knows-who or what. You can't stay here alone, two women with no men around," one of the guys said.

"Yes, we can. And are. No one will bother us. We've fished and fished and we will again. But not today. Granted, it beats fishing along the banks of Wills Creek but its still fishing. It's our vacation as well as yours and today, we're not going to fish.," I replied.

Seeing that we meant it they reluctantly loaded up the boats and left. Soon we girls were enjoying the quiet and solitude. We chatted, sunned, and read a bit.

Then, THEY came. A large canoe carrying two adults and what turned out to be ten little Indians. Soon we heard the wild blasts of horns as several taxis descended on the remote area.

It seems that once a month the government checks arrived and the cabs would transport the Indians to the nearest town for supplies. Soon there were more canoes. In other words, a lot of Indians. They pulled the crafts up on the shore and entered the cabs, taking their oars with them. Making sure we wouldn't steal them, I suppose.

We pretended to not notice them and they pretended to not notice us. Ignoring each other was rather difficult since we had inadvertently set up camp practically at their docking area. But after much scurrying about, finding spots in the cabs, they were gone and quiet settled in..

B.J. and I chatted and laughed about watching them stuffing themselves into those cabs, oars and heads sticking out of the windows. We enjoyed the rest of the day, doing little and enjoying the blessed quietness. Suddenly, in late afternoon, came the blasts of the taxi horns. Arriving in a cloud of dust and coming to a screeching halt, once again the Indians descended on us. They carried bags of supplies, toilet paper evidently being an important commodity. Some of them appeared to be a little inebriated. This time, a few even chose to greet us like we were old pals. Remember, the government checks had arrived and some sort of alcoholic beverages had evidently been on their lists of necessities. Maybe at the top of some lists. After all, it had been a cold, hard winter and…. well, never mind. One young man pointed to a young lady proclaiming his intentions to marry her. "Maybe tonight." he said slyly. The fella who had arrived earlier in the large canoe, as it turned out, was the chief. His canoe was the largest and had the only motor among several canoes. A very old and very noisy motor, but still a motor.

Now, the chief himself approached us with an invitation that we didn't find hard to resist. We were asked to join them that evening for a party. It seems that their children had recently returned from Quebec City, where they had attended school during the winter months and there was to be a celebration. A really big event. So big that they had killed a moose and some of the ladies were back at camp roasting

136 THE WILLS CREEK CHRONICLES

it. Shaking his head in disbelieve, the chief seemed to find it hard to understand how we could turn down his invitation.

But we did, graciously but firmly. Giving up on us, the old chief summoned his family. He and his wife shooed the tired, boisterous children into the canoe. Chaos erupted when grocery bags where added to the mix. The canoe sank deeper and deeper into the water. Frustrated, and more than a little drunk, the chief slammed the water with a large oar, splashing water over everyone. He yelled in a curious mixture of French, English and Ojibwa.

Ten little Indians scurried for land, returning one by one only after the screaming had subsided, a couple of them electing to catch a ride in another canoe. Finally, after getting everyone settled, they were ready to make the return trip home. But there was frustration over the lack of response from the old boat motor. After several tries, and much spitting and sputtering, the ancient thing came to life and the family headed across the lake.

Later, our families returned to camp and proudly showed off their catch of the day. Someone had caught the Big One, the largest any of us had caught in those waters. They were filled with stories of their adventures, chiding us for missing all the excitement.

When B.J and I were asked about our day; what went on, what did we do, we replied practically in unison, "Oh not much, just got in some R. and R." With that we girls started dinner while the men cleaned the best walleye you ever tasted. Straight from the cool, clear, uncontaminated waters of Grand Lake Victoria.

Later, after the children were tucked into their beds, the adults sat inside the dining fly, enjoying the evening and a cold beer. Northern Lights lit up the sky, a truly beautiful night. One of the men commented on the curious goings-on across the lake. What had been a Hudson Bay trading post was now the Indians summer camp and tonight, it was really jumping. "Never heard much from there before. There seems to be a lot of whooping and singing. And look at that big fire. Must be some sort of party," someone said.

B.J. and I, smiling to ourselves, agreed. "Yep, must be some sort of party."

Things were quiet across the lake the next day. We didn't see or hear much from the Indians, so B.J. and I determined that the big party that we had missed had probably turned out to be a howling success. Too bad we couldn't attend.

Oh, well. Maybe next year.

JOETTA VARANASI

Longhorn Meets The Settlers
A Gunshot Leads To An Ending He'd Never Imagined

Longhorn was a rebel who ran away from his Delaware Tribe when he was 14. He lived in a teepee on Wills Creek and had not spoken to anyone in five years, except the wild animals along Wills Creek. Growing up with his people taught him resourceful ways to survive, like fishing for food in the creek and using his bow and arrow to kill turkeys, rabbits, deer, and other wildlife he could use for food. His days were spent talking and playing with animals, picking wild berries and sharing them with his animal friends.

During the winter, Longhorn would rub sticks together to start a fire and huddle inside the teepee under the furs he brought with him when he left his tribe. Isolation made him even more savage, sometimes he let out loud war calls and loud screams.

One day he was screaming and beating on the drum his father had made him years ago. Happily entertaining himself and chanting to the beat of his drum, he never expected what was about to happen! A loud noise, like thunder, knocked him down against a tree. When he looked up, he was bleeding from his arm.

Feelings of confusion, anger, and shock entered his mind. He cried, "I must be shot." Remembering seeing a medicine man mend other Indians when he was a child gave him an idea about what to do next. He ran to the creek, washed the blood off and took distilled berry juice and poured it on the wound. After wrapping it tightly to stop the bleeding, he went inside of the teepee and slept.

The Bartright family had been traveling west on the Old National

Trail for days with two horses and a covered wagon. They reached what is now known, as East Cambridge and parked their wagon above the creek. Mr. Bartright and his son, Jeb, ventured down over the banks of Wills Creek to gather water and look for food. Mrs. Bartright took care of the baby and arranged their camp.

Longhorn was awakened by strange voices. Looking out of his teepee, he saw a white man and a little boy. For a moment, Longhorn was frightened. He wondered if they were the ones who shot him, as he watched them bathe in the clear waters and gather water from Wills Creek. As they were about to saddle their horses and ride away, the little boy noticed the teepee and yelled,

"Look, Daddy, over there, it's a teepee tent. Can we look in it? "Sure, son," replied the man. They moved toward Longhorn's teepee. He was so startled that his band of feathers fell off of his head to the ground. As he bent over to pick them up, the little boy reached for them at the same time. They made eye contact. The boy and his father noticed Longhorn's arm wrapped and leaking blood. Immediately, they wanted to help him. The older man went to his wagon, bringing back some whiskey, he removed the bullet and cleaned the wound.

They tried talking to Longhorn, but communication was difficult. Responding with thankful expressions and his warm eyes, Longhorn assured them he appreciated all they did to help. The family took Longhorn back to their wagon and continued to care for him. Mr. Bartright told him about how travel on the Old National Trial took days to arrive in Cambridge. Longhorn showed little Jeb how to use his bow and arrow, and let him wear his band of feathers. He wanted Mr. Bartright to have his knife as a gift. Longhorn, Mr. Bartright and Jeb were becoming friends fast.

One strange thing, though, when Mr. Bartright took a better look at the bullet he removed from Longhorn's arm, he recognized it as his own bullet. Yesterday while chasing a wild turkey, he had shot Longhorn by accident. He explained what had happened. Longhorn spoke in a broken language, "You my friend. Me you friend." Later they all sat down for an evening meal together.

In days to follow, Longhorn moved his teepee up high on the banks of Wills Creek to be near the Bartrights. He worked with them every day cutting trees and helping build a house. Later, they built a small house nearby for Longhorn. Since leaving his tribe, the little runaway Delaware Indian boy had found a new family.

PAM RITCHEY

LIGHTS OUT
Where Are Those Matches?

Jackie had been wracking her brain all evening trying to think of where she had seen the matches. The power outage, caused by a late summer storm, threatened to last several more hours, and she couldn't stand the thought of being alone in the dark again. She already checked the kitchen junk drawer, the linen closet and the buffet with no luck (other than a flashlight with dead batteries). Candles and oil lamps in almost every room, but since she quit smoking and thrown out her lighters, there was nothing to ignite that warm glow.

Evening shadows were deepening as she rummaged through the nightstand drawers. Nothing. She headed in to check the living room end tables. No luck there either. She glanced around what she usually considered a cozy room only to be startled by the shadow of the coat rack spreading its long arms on the opposite wall.

Trying to rein in her imagination as darkness filled the room, Jackie snuggled on the sofa. Suddenly lightening streaked through the darkness outlining the shadow of a man in the kitchen window. She sat in stunned silence straining to catch a glimpse of the shadow again. Was her mind once more playing tricks?

Slowly she slipped to the floor and cautiously made her way on all fours to the kitchen archway. Panic swelled within her chest as she heard the rattle of the knob on the back door.

Turning and pressing her back against the wall, Jackie's mind raced trying to find a way to get help. The storm had knocked out cell phone service along with the electric, so she had no working phone to call 911.

Bright lights and a knock at the front door made her heart pound even harder. "Jackie, are you home?" came after the next set of knocks.

The familiar voice of her neighbor, Jeff, brought Jackie to her feet in an instant. Racing to the door, she swung it open crying out about the man trying to get in her back door.

"No, No, it was me! I'm sorry for scaring you so badly. You know how scared my dog Mutt is of thunder. Well he ran off after a big clap. I saw him on your back porch, but right as I got close he jumped on your door then took off towards Wills Creek. I went over and turned on my truck lights then came over here to ask if you could help look for him. I'm so sorry," Jeff said."

"That's okay," Jackie said between tension-easing bursts of laughter. "Let's go look for him. By the way, do you have any matches?"

DONA McCONNELL

Maggie's Lesson
A "Head Case" Turns A Couple's Heads

Rachael Hobbs flinched as the back door slammed with an ear-splitting boom. Maggie, she knew instantly. Who else believed that a door had to be slammed before it could be locked? And an unlocked door was not an option for Maggie.

"Lots of weird-os out there," she always said. Except in her Mississippi voice it came out "weer-ed-o's."

Rachael knew that her husband Brian, working at home today, would be fuming. He abhorred everything about Molly, from her constant man bashing to her "last word" pronouncements on every subject. "A real head case," Brian said. "A walking cliche."

Still, Maggie was the best housekeeper Rachael ever had, the only one who took the mess created by two teenaged daughters in stride. Between Rachael's career as a swing shift RN and her husband's booming investment business, that was a Godsend. It was clear Maggie thought the Hobbs family was a short evolutionary step above pigs when it came to housekeeping. ("Cleanliness, you know, honey, next to Godliness," she'd remind Rachael.)

"Gotta get busy," Maggie said. "Duane's turkey huntin' at dark, and he'll be screaming for early supper." Maggie's face clouded. "Don't know about him, Miz Hobbs. Too fussy. Bossy, like. If he wasn't number four, I'd be bootin' him." Rachael turned away with a smile. She had heard it all before.

Number one was before her time, but according to Molly he was "too fain-ciful and air-headed. Good dresser, but "couldn't figger out how to start a weed eater."

144 THE WILLS CREEK CHRONICLES

Number two was too lazy. "Wouldn't hit a lick at a snake," according to Maggie. He had lasted just four months. "Laziness in a man's like them bouquets of store-bought flares. They look good, but what do you really need 'em for?

Number three had too many bad habits. "Smoked like a tar kiln," Maggie said. Seeing Rachael's quizzical look, she explained in a voice reserved for the very young or very slow. "Like when you got a lot of old tars and you want to burn 'em.' You make a little kiln and that rubber smoke is so thick and black it'll dang near choke you to death."

Rachel finally understood that it was tires, not tar, although she was now so confused it didn't really matter.

Duane, number four, or "current" as she often called him, was "too grabby. "What do men thank they buy for the cost of a blood test, anyway?" Maggie said. Four had lasted the longest, so far. Apparently, "grabbiness" was a bearable trait, at least temporarily. "He does have a saucy smile," Maggie reflected. Each divorce had required a small advance ("Jus' to git me back on my feet") and, before you knew it, the next candidate was up for possible election into Maggie's personal "Hall of Temporary Matrimony."

"Why marry them, Maggie?" Rachael had asked one day. "Why not just live together?"

"Wouldn't they like that?" Maggie said, obviously horrified. "Gitt'n the milk for free without buyin' the cow! Plus, that's a mortal sin. Don't you know 'nothin' about religion, honey?"

Rachael kept quiet. She questioned why four marriages didn't trouble Molly's ethical sensibilities, but it was really none of her business.

"'Sides, I'm a pure romantic, yes I am. Duane, my current, had the moves. Got me like a June bug with one foot in a spider web, shakin' and rattlin' to get out, but just gettin' in tighter. He was a charmin' one, that Duane."

As Rachael looked up, she exchanged glances with her husband Brian, who was clearly listening from the office. To him, Molly's endless pronouncements were like chalk on a blackboard.

"Besides, you gotta' have a man, right? Woman without a man's like a cow without a cud. Pitiful, she is."

MAGGIE'S LESSON **145**

Brian sat at his desk, two index fingers pointed at himself, reminding Rachael of her good fortune.

"Still," Rachael plowed on. "To have so many disappointments...."

"Oh, Hell," Maggie said. "That's just men, honey. They ain't nothin' but disappointment. Just like bottle rockets. They start out with a bang, then fizzle out before you hardly get to enjoy 'em."

Rachael looked back toward Brian with a smirk. He pretended to be concentrating on his work.

Grabbing up loose clothes with both hands, a well-oiled cleaning machine, Maggie plowed forward. "Like last night," she said. "I'm doin' two things at once, tryin' to cook plus wrenching my hair out in the sink - you know how I like to look good for work."

Rachael glanced at the ragged jeans and frayed t-shirt. She did spend time on her hair which was, well, complicated. Swooshes and swirls circled her head, ending in a bouffant parade of curls across the front. Her reverie was interrupted by Maggie's tirade.

"Then, glory be, here come the hands, just a grabbin'. While I'm tryin' to wrench out my hair! Made me madder 'n forty Hells.

In the office, where Rachael couldn't resist glancing, Brian hand two hand 's full of hair, mimicking the literal idea of "wrenching" hair. She muffled a giggle.

Maggie was from Southern Mississippi, which Brian said was a waste of two words when one would do. She had grown up in the country, where she learned a strong work ethic and a lack of tolerance for "trifflin-ness," a word she used to describe anything imprctical or useless. A lot of things in Maggie's world were deemed "pure trifflin'ness."

Rachael was startled by Maggie's next question. "So, honey, how's things with you and your man?"

"Well, uh, fine, I suppose," Rachael stammered.

"Humm, I see," said Maggie knowingly.

"No, fine, really," said Rachael.

The truth was, Rachael and Brian had been having a rough patch. They didn't seem to laugh much these days, and their love life was practically non-existent. Busy schedules rarely allowed meals together, and long romantic dinners were a pre-parent memory. Rachael had brushed it aside as the price of having two careers and two teenagers.

146 THE WILLS CREEK CHRONICLES

Today was a rare occasion, when both were home at the same time, even if only for a few hours. But, of course, Brian was engrossed in his work, oblivious to her presence. Working, always working.

"You know, honey, men are like maple trees," Maggie began. "They get all dried up. Need some priming sometimes if you want the sap to start flowing again."

Rachel sensed rather than saw Brian's attention.

"Priming." Rachael said.

"You know, a little booster shot to the ego and you might get a booster shot of your own," Maggie winked. Rachel's gaping mouth was her only response. In his office, Brian was making a typically male gesture that could be characterized, at the very least, as "triflin'."

"Honey, ain't no wonder you've been stuck with one husband all these years," Maggie said sympathetically. "You don't seem to know nothin' about men. See, they like to think they're all strong and tough, but they're just like big coconuts. They got their hard man-shells on the outside. But break 'em open and what's inside is soft and stringy. You got to look close and decide if the inside part is worth the trouble of scrapin' it out."

Brian's office door slammed with a vengeance.

Rachael was slighly alarmed to realize Maggie was actually making sense. She marveled at the simplicity with which Maggie seemed to mange her life. Althought it seemed a mess to others, it clearly made perfect sense to her. And she seemed far happier than Rachael herself, despite little money, a tiny house in a cheap neighborhood and a future that promised minimal luxuries.

Rachael found herself following Maggie around as she cleaned, hungry for clues to her own happiness.

"Sweets, let's sit down a sec. I need to eat my sandwich. My sugar's droppin' and I'm so hungry I could eat the butt out of a rag doll."

Rachael made coffee and they sat together at the table, two impossibly different women with a universal commonality – their men.

Tentatively, Rachael asked, "Maggie how do you keep your husbands, uh, husband interested."

"Well, honey, it's the simplest three-letter word in the diction'ry."

Of course, that's what Maggie would say. Blushing, Rachael braced for the explanation.

"Eye," Maggie continued.

"Eye?" Rachael said, now thoroughly stymied.

"You got to look 'em in the eye," Maggie continued. Did you ever see them young couples at a restaurant? They never stop looking into each other's eyes. It's like they're drinkin' each other. Then you look at the ole married ones. They talk, but they never look each other in the eye. If you don't look your man in the eye, I mean a long, drinkin' look, you ain't really talkin' to him. Every little thing he's thinkin' and feelin' is in his eyes. His whole insides is in there. Yours, too. You'd be amazed how people forgets that."

Rachael was stunned. She remembered the days when she couldn't take her eyes off Brian, when she couldn't tell you what she had eaten, only what Brian had said. How long since she really looked at him? Could a basket case like Maggie actually be right?

"Well, back to work," Maggie said. "Sittin' here ain't buying the baby no shoes nor payin' for the ones he's got."

Maggie left the room in a blur of abundant hair and pungent cleaning supplies. Rachael continued to sit at the table, pondering. A movement from the doorway caught her attention. Brian was standing there, looking at her intently. His face was a mixture of sadness and resolve.

"Hey there," he said.

"Hi, honey, how's it going?"

She suddenly noticed that Brian was looking directly into her eyes. The effect made her nervous and twittery. What was wrong with her?

"So, how about a date tonight?" He continued his intense stare. Obviously, he had overheard Maggie's lesson on love.

"But the girls"...she stammered.

"The girls are nearly grown," Brian said. "Besides, they've got the world's most expensive cell phones if they need us."

Rachael looked directly into his eyes. "Why, I'd love to go on a date."

Maggie never understood why she got a whopping raise the next week when she didn't do a thing than different the week before.

"Rich people," she muttered to herself. "Ain't got the sense God gave a goose."

LINDA BURRIS

WILLS CREEK WEDDING
It Started Along The Creek And Ended At The Altar

It's a hot summer day along Wills Creek. The Young Life group and their advisers, Tim and Cindy Parks, are looking forward to this time of fun and fellowship.

Woods of oak and maple trees surround their campsite on three sides with the creek on the east side. Putting up the two tents and finding wood for their campfire keeps the campers busy until supper time. With darkness fast approaching, Cindy and the girls begin to use two-pronged wooden sticks to roast the hot dogs and marshmallows, while Tim and the boys gather more wood for the campfire.

Sally and the girls asked, "Let's sing some campfire songs. How about Kumbayah or some of the choruses we sing at church?"

Tim and Cindy led the group in choruses for a while but the group was still restless. "Remember the last camp-out? You completely freaked out when the wind picked up and the leaves swirled around the clearing and the clouds covered the full moon. You ran into your tent screaming as if you had seen a ghost," chortled Billy.

"I did see a ghost beside the creek! It was on it's knees lapping at the water," Sally said.

Billy laughed, "Remember that ghost turned out to be a dirty, straggly thirsty dog."

"What do you suggest we do?" asked Cindy.

"Since there are so many stars out tonight, let's stargaze before we go to our tents. The twinkling stars are beautiful, just like fireworks on the fourth of July," said Cindy.

They looked up and pointed out some familiar constellations: North Star, Big Dipper, Little Dipper and several others. "Okay, said Tim, time for bed."

The babbling of the creek and the soft breeze among the trees lulled them into a peaceful night's sleep.

Billy and Sally started seeing more and more of each other during the summer and looked forward to their senior year of high school. Sally was on the cheerleading squad and Billy played as running back on the football team. They saw each other often at their cheerleading and football practices before school started the last week of August. After the Friday night football games, cheerleaders and football players went to the Willow Diner to re-hash the game. Sally and Billy sat together and joined in the usually hilarious summation of the game. They went together to school and church activities, too.

Before they knew it their senior year at Willow High was almost over, only graduation remained. During the summer, working and dating lasted until Billy went to the state university on a football scholarship. Sally worked part-time at the diner and went to the community college to study nursing. The two wrote letters until he came home for the holidays. They had grown serious in their relationship during their time apart, even talking about marriage someday.

Billy and Sally one winter's evening went for a walk along ice-covered Wills Creek. The trees were laden with soft, downy snow. Stopping by the creek, Billy took Sally's gloved hands, looked at her golden, blonde hair and into her blue eyes solemnly as he could and said, " Sally, we have known each other since kindergarten. We have shared our lives and at Young Life. You are my one and only love. Will you marry me?"

Sally looked into his deep-set dark eyes to answer softly and solemnly and replied, "Yes Billy, I'll be honored to be your wife for now and ever. Since we're in our first year of college our parents will want us to wait until we graduate to get married."

"I agree to go by their suggestions," said Billy.

Their parents suggested they wait until their graduations from college. Their wedding date was set for June the first after their graduation. They wanted their wedding in their special place along Wills Creek with the reception at the Elks Lodge in Willow.

Before their wedding by the creek, the birds were singing and even the creek was gurgling its approval. There were puffy, white clouds in the sky. The clearing was dominated by an arch covered by red, white and yellow roses entwined with sprigs of ivy. A violinist played the wedding march as Sally and her father approached the arch. Rev. Scott, the maid of honor and best man stood behind the arch. Sally and Billy entered the arch to exchange their vows and wedding rings.

"Sally, will you become my wife and mother of our children? I will be your husband and provider. I pledge my love, and faithfulness to you now and forever." Sally looked into his face and said "Yes."

Then she looked into Billy's eyes and asked, " Billy, will you be my husband and father of our children? I will be your wife and companion. I pledge my love and faithfulness for the rest of our lives." Billy gazed into Sally's eyes, "Yes," he said softly. They exchanged wedding rings. Rev. Scott pronounced them husband and wife, and Billy lifted her veil and kissed her.

Sally loved Billy's red 1965 Ford Mustang convertible, which was driven by Billy's brother to the reception, with the newlyweds in the back seat. Later they danced the first dance together after which Sally danced with her father. "Honey, I can't believe you are married. Seems like yesterday we were going fishing down at the creek. You loved to fish and play in the sparkling water," her father said.

Sally looked into her father's face and said, "That little girl is all grown up. The years have gone by so fast. I'll miss you and mom and the home where I grew up," she replied.

Their wedding cake was white trimmed with blue icing with the traditional bride and groom on top. Billy took the blue garter off of Sally's leg and tossed it towards the single men. Sally then tossed her bridal bouquet toward the single women. Then they thanked everyone for being with them on this special day and left for their honeymoon at Dailey's Bed and Breakfast about 20 miles from where they were married up Wills Creek.

At sunset they took a walk beside the creek. They held hands, looked into each others faces and pledged to love each other for ever and ever.

SAMUEL D. BESKET

The Embezzler
A Financial Adviser He Wasn't

Walking into Clint's office, Mr. Moore laid the negotiable bonds on his desk. "I can't stress enough the importance of registering these today. Try not to screw them up."

Mr. Moore turned and started for the door, stopping halfway he paused, "Carolyn and I are expecting you and Beth for dinner tonight. We're having a few friends over. Please be on time."

"Yes sir." Clint replied. Mr. Moore (Tom) was Clint's father-in-law. Shaking his head Tom walked out without saying good bye.
Starring at the bonds Clint pondered the last five years. Marrying the boss's daughter seemed like a good idea back then, but things hadn't worked out the way he had hoped. Several of his trades resulted in huge losses for the firm. Since then he had been assigned trivial work, normally assigned to an office assistant.

Then there was Beth, 50 pounds heavier than when they married. Her only interest was being daddy's girl. God, how he would like to escape this prison, but he had grown accustomed to this life-style. It's a long way from the banks of Wills Creek to New York.

After dinner that evening everyone broke up into small groups to talk. Suddenly, Tom motioned for Clint to come into his private office. Wow, this can't be good Clint thought.

Pointing to a chair in the corner, Tom handed him a list of clients. "I'm taking Carolyn on a two-week cruise for our fortieth anniversary. I need to keep in touch with these clients." I'll need you to fax me all correspondence on this list to the ship, since I won't have access to a computer. The password for my personnel computer is DEH85; it gives you access to all the firm's clients. Be careful not to compromise it. By the way, I asked Beth to join us. If you need help, ask my personal assistant, Brittany."

Walking out of Tom's office Clint thought, Wow, another mundane job, copying messages off the boss's computer. Motioning to Beth that he was ready to leave, Clint winked at Carolyn. "Dinner was great. Enjoy your vacation."

Driving home Clint thought of the next two weeks. "Things should be quiet with Tom gone," he muttered. "Now, if I could get rid of Brittany I would have it made." He couldn't figure out how she moved up so fast to be Tom's assistant.

Things were slow at the office the following week. Clint faxed several transactions to the ship. Scanning through Tom's files, he noticed a file that kept popping up that wasn't on the list. T&B Investments. Curiosity finally got the best of him and he opened it. Reading through the file Clint couldn't believe what he was seeing. Huge amounts of money were being transferred to a private account in the Cayman Islands for Brittany with Tom as the sponsor.

What's going on, Clint thought. Why is Tom funding an account in the Cayman's for Brittany? Why is he using the firm's money? With current bond prices at an all time high it is worth over six million dollars.

Later that evening, Clint couldn't get the thought out of his mind. Could Tom and Brittany be having an affair? That would explain how she moved up so fast in the firm. But Tom? School board president, and a deacon in the church? How could he do this?

The next morning Clint was set to confront Brittany about the secret account. Sitting at his desk he noticed a letter addressed to him from Brittany. "Clint, I'm taking a week's vacation in the Cayman Islands. Tom said it was OK."

So that's it, Clint thought. Tom and Carolyn's ship is stopping there this week. I bet he's going to cash out and skip the country."
Leaning back in his chair Clint thought. Well, that makes things a lot clearer. I know why Tom has been meeting with the company lawyers and all his stock transfers. He's not coming back. Clint couldn't get his mind off what he had just found out.

Picking up his briefcase, he walked out. "I'll be home if anyone needs me," he told the receptionist. I just can't believe it, Clint thought. Tom built this company from scratch, and now he is going to throw it away for a 22 year old floozie. Who would believe me if I blew the whistle?

Playing with dinner at a local diner that evening, Clint couldn't keep his mind off the account. Crazy thoughts entered his mind. It would be so easy to sell the bonds and transfer the money to his account and skip the country. Tom couldn't turn him in without exposing himself. After all, he had the password. But where would he go?

"Would you like a paper to read?" the waitress asked as she filled his coffee cup.

"Thanks, I can use a distraction."

Bold headlines covered the top of the paper, "Government Fails In Bid To Extradite Don Bros. From Mallett Islands." He remembered how those brothers ran the largest Ponzi scheme this country had ever seen. Reading further, the paper stated how government attorneys were returning to the Cayman Islands after failing to reach an agreement on extradition.

Walking to his car, Clint spotted the headlines again at a news stand. That has to be it, he thought. He's going to skip. It's too perfect a plan to be coincidental. Now, I know why he wanted Beth to go along; he doesn't want to leave Carolyn alone.

Later that day Clint decided to sell the bonds and transfer the money to his account once he was in the islands. A lot safer that way, he thought. No time for someone to check on it. Then he would set up an account for Carolyn and give her half. Then comes the hard part; telling Carolyn what he had found out about Tom and Brittany.

The next day Clint made plans to leave without arousing suspicion. Need to make this look like a business trip, he thought. "Book me on the first flight to Miami tomorrow," Clint told the receptionist. "I have some urgent business to take care of."

Sipping his drink that evening Clint called Carolyn's cell phone. "I have some exciting news for you. I don't want to tell Tom or Beth yet. I'm flying in tomorrow; can you meet me in the bar in the Hilton on Grand Cayman West, say about seven in the evening?"

After a short pause Carolyn answered, "Sure Clint, sure. But why

154 THE WILLS CREEK CHRONICLES

can't I tell Tom? We never keep secrets from each other."

"This is too big, Carolyn, too big."

"Well, I guess," she replied. "We could use some good news. I suppose you know Brittany is here."

"Yeah, she left me a note, and thanks for trusting me, good night."

"Good night, Clint."

The flight to Miami was routine. Clint booked his own flight to the Caymans with connections to the Mallet Islands. Prior to leaving Miami, he changed his mind again and transferred the bonds from Tom's account to a new one he set up for himself in the Caymans. By the time the market opens tomorrow, I'll be gone, he thought.

Arriving early Thursday morning, Clint thought, Why didn't I say noon instead of 7 p.m.? I'm not good at waiting.

Ordering a beer for himself and a vodka tonic for Carolyn, he waited. As usual she was on time. Kissing him on the cheek, Carolyn said, "I've been worried sick, what's so important that we have to meet in secret?"

"Sit down, we have to talk." Over the next hour Clint told Carolyn what he found out, and what he had done, all the time Carolyn was sobbing and shaking her heat. "Clint, Clint," she said. "I guess we should have told you."

"Told me what?"

"This is hard for me," Carolyn replied, starring at her drink. "Let me explain. Tom is Brittany's father."

"Brittany's father!," Clint shouted.

Carolyn continued. "After college graduation, Tom and some friends got drunk. Tom and a friend, Sue, got married. She was Jewish and Tom is Irish Catholic. After her parents found out, they had the marriage annulled. What Tom didn't know was, Sue was pregnant. They never told him. Sue's parents raised Brittany as their own child. Things were fine until a few years ago when Brittany developed a rare blood disease. They had to tell Brittany the truth, and called Tom. The doctors told them a blood transfusion from her biological father will cure the disease. Clint, Clint, are you OK?"

Clint looked catatonic. Sobbing, Carolyn went into all the details. "There's more. We took this cruise to tell Beth she has a half-sister, and to get the treatment here in the islands. I'm sorry about all the secrecy. We should have spoken up sooner."

"It's OK, it's OK," Clint replied excitedly. "I, ah, I can fix it. I'll buy the bonds back, delete the transaction and no one will know."

"Too late, too late," sobbed Carolyn. "T&B Security called Tom the minute you sold the bonds. You broke two laws, Clint. Money in a 259 bond account can only be sold with Tom's approval. And you did the transaction outside the country. Furthermore, Tom didn't embezzle the money; it was an inheritance from his father. "I can't believe you did this."

Motioning toward a table next to them, Carolyn continued, "Those two fellows are from the Treasury Department. They want to talk to you."

Clint placed his head on his hands on the table.

"I'll be outside," Carolyn said.

Walking toward the door she heard one of the treasury agents say, "Mr. Rae, could we have a word with you?"

MARILYN DURR

Needed: One Good Driver
Bank Robberies Don't Always Go As Planned

Maxine and David Carlucci kept a welcome mat on the front porch of their west Florida home. Unexpected guests weren't unusual— during decent hours. Tonight would be different. Frantic pounding on their front door at a quarter past midnight interrupted a quiet night.

Being roused from blissful sleep didn't phase Maxine. She loved entertaining any time, day or night, which exasperated her husband. Dave, on the other hand, was waist-deep in a fantastic dream about bikini-clad beauties on a deserted island in the south Pacific. He maintained an air of unexplainable irritation as he scrambled for his clothes.

"There's a police car with flashing lights in our driveway— and we're out of snacks." Maxine, donning her prettiest robe, ran nimble fingers through her messy hair. "Where's the microwave popcorn, Dave? We have guests."

"Just answer the door, Max, the police aren't here for snacks." Dave stumbled into the living room, pulling his jeans over long legs and grumbling loudly. "Stupid welcome mat. Either we bring it in every night, or I'm moving back to the banks of Wills Creek in Ohio." Dave's face reeked crabbiness. His jeans were on backwards and were quite uncomfortable, intensifying his grumpiness.

Maxine opened the door, carrying a two-day-old bag of leftover microwave popcorn. An officer stood at attention on their porch with his hand resting on his holstered gun.

"Ma'am, I'm Officer Duncan. Sorry to wake you, but we have a situation."

"Oh, how thrilling. I'm Maxine Carlucci... this is my husband David, Dave for short. Would you like some popcorn? It's buttered you know. A situation? What kind? Are you sure you won't have some buttery popcorn?"

"No thank you, I'm on duty. Regulations forbid buttery. Three bank robbers... in your lake. Seems the driver lost control and their getaway car slammed into the water."

"How rude. Should I put on some make-up?" Maxine, twittering about like a lovesick love-bug, appeared a tad unstable to Dave and Officer Duncan. Her eyes were glowing. "Say, do you rent your bullets? Do you get them back after you shoot criminals?"

"Make more popcorn while Officer Duncan and I talk, Max. Sorry, she's excitable when we're out of snacks."

"Mr. Carlucci, we'll need to be on this side of your lake to apprehend three perpetrators if they swim to shore."

"That's not likely, Officer Duncan." Dave's voice was stern, but he smothered a laugh.

"Why's that, sir?"

"It's not a good idea to feed alligators. Besides, 'gators get heartburn when they eat criminals, and that makes them cranky. You can't get along with them when they're cranky."

"My family and dogs swim in the far end of your lake. I've never seen any alligators." Officer Duncan turned pale.

"Ahhh— well, unless you want to become Florida Snack Crackers, I suggest you find another swimming hole." Feeling devilish, Dave grinned at Officer Duncan, adding, "Your bank robbers better stay right where they are or they'll end up criminal crunchies."

Officer Duncan radioed this surprising information to his commanding officer. A scratchy, nervous voice crackled over the radio, "Ask Carlucci how many and how big? Where do they nest?"

"Sebastian's eight feet or better and Trixie, the dainty one, is between six and seven feet I'd guess. That's what Maxine named them, incidentally—I'm partial to Thelma and Louise, and now they have their very own car. Just like in the movie. Three crooks probably won't fill them up, but you add a couple of cops to the mix and it might do the trick. They nest wherever they want."

Dave and Max settled into their lounge chairs close to a swarm of law enforcement officials scurrying back and forth along the shoreline of their tiny lake. From this spot, they could hear the police jargon being bandied about.

Dave's alligator information caused lengthy discussions between the local police, the sheriff's department and FBI.

"How do we take the suspects into custody without becoming edible guests at an alligator buffet?" asked a deputy.

"Won't the 'gators be out of sorts because a little red car made a splash-landing smack in the middle of their home? How will we get around them to execute a rescue? " a police officer asked.

"I would say very carefully," said Dave as he chortled at the sight of three nervous criminals sitting on top of the car.

A question arose from a sheriff's deputy, "What are the legalities if we leave the perps where they landed?"

"We'll lose the money as well as the alleged robbers. That won't do, the money's important," answered an FBI agent. Dave rubbed his hands together, still chortling.

A bull-horn appeared and an FBI man made an announcement, "Stay quiet, there are alligators in the lake. We're calling for a boat to rescue the money...er, you."

Max and Dave munched buttery popcorn on their side of the narrow lake, snickering as bank robbers launched into panic screaming and tussling for higher ground on the car's roof. Dave and Maxine heard the bad guys yell, "We'll stay where we are, we don't wanna be shredded up 'turkey' salad."

One robber said to the others in a high-pitched voice, "Front-page headlines are better if we're around to enjoy them."

Dave watched the ghostly underwater glow emanating from the car's headlights. "Those oversized 'gators are sure enticed," he said to Max.

"They're getting real close and personal." They laughed when one of the bank robbers cried out, "I think the big one has a napkin around his neck."

Dave knew it wasn't a sure thing because shadows cast by eerie fluorescence were deceiving. To make matters worse, the alligators floated back and forth as if waiting for a tasty morsel of bad guy to slide kicking and shrieking into their mouths.

Another anxious robber yelled, "Hey, get us out of here. Those 'gators are licking their chops."

Dave punched Maxine's arm, laughing hilariously. "Gators enjoy a challenge and some fight in their meals."

"Yeah, and this meal has real potential," Max said, giggling around a mouthful of popcorn. "Unfortunately for the bank robbers, there aren't any rescue boats available," the sheriff said. "The FBI called a local boat owner who got angry at being awakened in the middle of the night. He'll be here, but it'll take him an hour and a half to arrive on scene."

"He only lives two blocks away," Dave snickered to Officer Duncan.

Once the boat owner appeared, the Carluccis heard the stranded criminals cheer, "We're going to be arrested with all our body parts intact."

"Hey. Is that supposed to be a boat? It looks like a slab of floating boards. It can't be more than a couple of two-by-fours held together with thread," one of the criminals cried.

Dave couldn't resist taunting the crooks. "Shaky little lumber pile to get rescued with, eh, boys? Sure wouldn't inspire my confidence."

Screaming and yelling commenced from the car's rooftop island. "We have to ride in that thing? What if it sinks? Can't you find a bigger one? We'll wait— order a real boat."

Dave saw the tension on the law enforcement officers' faces as they argued over which poor souls would volunteer to row the boat, save the money, take the thieves into custody, and fasten a tow truck cable to the submerged car.

"I can understand why no one wants to rush headlong into a rescue," Dave said. Maxine nodded, her mouth too full of buttery popcorn to speak.

Meanwhile, the Carluccis listened to increasingly hysterical bank robbers fighting, they assumed, over who'd be saved first. An oarsman and a brave deputy armed with a high-powered weapon to dispatch hungry alligators if needed, held two of three places on the boat.

"There isn't enough room left for a pair of handcuffs in that bobbing hunk of driftwood," Dave told Maxine, her eyes sparkling as she crammed two hefty handfuls of popcorn in her mouth.

Spotlights illuminated the water. Trixie was larger than the boat, which caused fighting to escalate on the car roof, evolving from swearing and yelling to shoving. A foot slipped into the water, a 'gator moved in for his kill, the oarsman stopped rowing and the deputy raised his weapon ready for action if the alligators tried for a free lunch.

Excitement sent electrical type currents through Dave, "Finally some real action."

A bull-horn cackled and screeched to life as a gruff voice announced,

"If you don't cease and desist all sound and movement, operations will halt."

Another voice, one of many spectators, bellowed, "Shoot 'em where they sit."

"Dave, this is better than any movie." Maxine's bumpy, chipmunk cheeks were being stuffed with buttery popcorn in pell-mell fashion, making it hard to understand her breathless words. "Best of all, it's free," she sputtered. Bits and pieces of wet corn spewed from her mouth in globs.

"Free, sure, if you don't count the cost of bug spray, drinks and popcorn, Max." Dave was still somewhat testy about losing his heartthrob dream.

Calm returned and the rescue continued in a slow, cautious manner until the first bank robber screamed, "The boat's leaking. We're gonna die, we're gonna die. Help." This raised a cacophony of ranting plus major ridicule from observers lining the shore.

Someone in the midst of the crowd cried out, "Next time put an ad in the classifieds — Needed: One good driver for get-a-way car. Must know how to drive."

Finally, the third culprit landed on solid ground. "Can someone roll up the car windows and turn off the headlights? I'm afraid if they're left on they'll run my battery down and I'll have to buy a new one," he said.

Officer Duncan laughed heartily, Dave was in stitches and Maxine turned blue from hysterical laughter.

"This guy isn't as bright as the lights on his car will be in a few hours. Roll up the windows. Ha! Does he think it's going to rain and get the water inside his car wet?" Dave chuckled. "Maybe he thinks crooks are allowed to take their cars to prison. Well, he was the one driving the get-a-way car, wasn't he?"

Max and Dave gathered up their chairs and trash. He grabbed Maxine's free hand as they walked toward their house and said, "This turned out to be a fun-filled evening, honey."

"Yes it did, Dave. I love spending quality time with my husband. The buttery popcorn made the whole evening." They both laughed.

"I don't think I'll move back to the banks of Wills Creek after all, Max."

JERRY WOLFROM

❦

THE ECHO OF LITTLE KATE
The Greatest Foxhound That Ever Lived

Return with me now to the middle-1930's when my father moved us to the hills of northern Guernsey County near meandering Wills Creek. The social life there centered on the pot-bellied stove at the ramshackle Knox Brothers Sawmill not far from Kimbolton. There were about 15 houses in the community, occupied by hard-working, friendly folks. Mostly timber men and coal miners, they named the settlement Knoxtown. I was about seven.

Nearly every man in the area was a devout fox hunter, each with several well-bred fox hounds. They never killed the fox; they just loved to hear the pack chase them in "full cry" until the fox "went aground." Knoxtown was nestled in the Wills Creek valley, anchored on all four sides by high hills. Once a week, winter and summer, the fox hunters would select a hilltop site and turn the hounds loose. After that, they sat by a campfire to sip coffee and listened to the mountain music of the hounds giving chase.

"Old Drum's in the lead," Moss Blymyer would exclaim proudly.

"Yeah, but my Rowdy and Bess ain't far behind," John Clymer would respond.

The competition and amicable arguing would go on all night. "Sounds like your old Buster has quit," Arnold Keller would say to Byron Keel.

"Buster's getting old."

"Hey, Jack, your Rock is off on a deer again."

"Rock never ran a deer in his life."

THE ECHO OF LITTLE KATE **163**

Each hound had a distinctive voice when they gave chase. Some were bawlers, some choppers. Put them together and you had a beautiful cacophony that excited even the townspeople who could hear the echoing chorus from their front porches on warm nights.

It didn't take Dad long to acquire a foxhound. He drove to Spratt see to a well-known English foxhound breeder, but was disappointed to find the man had only one pup left from a litter of eight. The man gave Dad the female because she was the runt of the litter, but she was perfectly marked--white, brown and black.

The veteran hunters shook their heads when they saw Little Kate, but they were too courteous to tell dad that she wouldn't amount to much. Just not large enough or strong enough to run with the big dogs. Little Kate slept in a warm dog house outside but Dad often allowed her inside to bond with the family. She was always well-behaved and loveable. Little Kate became something of a pet–a different little gal with a contagious personality.

When she was ten months old, it was time for her first hunt. Not much happened that night, but Little Kate, running well back in the pack, did emit sharp, lyrical bawls, surprisingly loud for a beginner. As the months wore on, she worked her way to the front of the pack, and by the time she was two, she was an out and out leader. Even the Knoxtown observers sitting outside their houses, quickly learned to recognize her golden-tone voice as it reverberated against the hills. She soon became the darling of the area, partly because of her brassy bawl, partly because she stuck with a track longer than the rest of the pack.

As the night wore on, most of the hounds would "run themselves out," finally limping slowly back to the campfire. But not Little Kate who by that time had developed unusual speed. Cass Bixel called her Cinder Foot.

One day a fox hunter from Illinois came through town and heard the stories of Little Kate's voice and perseverance. He offered Dad seventy-five dollars for her, no trial needed. An enormous sum but Little Kate wasn't for sale at any price.

While there were four different hilltops where the fox hunters could station themselves, knowing they could always strike a fox track, they never went to the Cribbs Section because it was too close

164 THE WILLS CREEK CHRONICLES

to Route 21, a main artery used by big trucks rolling north to Canton, and south to Cambridge. Trucks presented extreme danger to hounds. One crisp, fall evening, after villagers turned out in force to enjoy a wiener roast behind the saw mill, the fox hunters headed for White Eyes Ridge to put on a show. Villagers, along with fox hunters from several parts of Guernsey County, sat around the hot dog fire embers to enjoy the chase. As usual, Little Kate made the first strike, and the chase was on. The entire valley came alive with the sound of excited hounds on a hot trail. It was a red fox, not a gray, the hunters reckoned, because red foxes cast a wider circle than grays.

The chase continued for two hours when Clem Taggert muttered, "Uh, oh! "They're over in the Cribbs Section. The red flag went up. Clem grabbed his bugle, a hollowed-out steer horn, and began to call in the dogs. One at a time the tired hounds returned to the campfire. But Little Kate stuck to the track all by herself. By her excited bawls ringing across the valley, the guys knew she was closing in on the fox and wouldn't give up until her quarry went aground.

Even the spectators below were extremely worried, and when Little Kate's bawl stopped, a hush fell over them. Dad and his friends waited for two hours at their hilltop campfire, but Little Kate never came in. Fearing the worst, Dad and his friends headed for Rt. 21. Sure enough, just west of North Salem, they discovered Little Kate's lifeless body on the berm, the casualty of a passing truck. There was a sad hush at the Knoxtown fire circle when Dad removed Little Kate's broken form from the trunk of his car.

The community had lost a close friend.

The following day the guys took Little Kate to the top of Lambert's Ridge, where she was laid to rest with some final words from Rev. Ralph McVey, a fox hunter himself. "We will never forget that wonderful voice as Little Kate led the pack over hill and dale," he said tearfully. "We'll never hear such music again."

Dad never bought another fox hound and I grieved for weeks after Little Kate left us. That winter, some townspeople said they could step outside on frosty, moonlit nights and hear Little Kate's unforgettable voice echoing across the White Eyes Valley.

Since then–seventy years later-- when the moon is full and the wind just right, I can hear that little angel in full cry, her brassy bawls ricocheting across the hilltops. I gaze skyward toward the full moon set against twinkling stars, and tears come to my eyes when I faintly hear Little Kate's thrilling voice in some far-off place singing with the Heavenly Choir.

RICHARD A. DAIR

Crazy Sally
She Headed West Into Unforgiving Territory

*U*nhappy with the way civilization was heading, and although a woman, Sally Rominger left the relative safety and security of her home in Cambridge Ohio and headed west. Into the unknown where only the toughest and fearless dared to tread. It was there she found freedom and the love of her life.

Long before sunrise, Crazy Sally had crawled out of bed. She stoked the fire, put on a pot of coffee and prepared for the long day ahead. Dressing in her homemade deerskins over male red long johns she quickly packed a cold sandwich of crusty sourdough bread and deer jerky slathered with a generous amount of lard she had rendered from the bear she shot in the fall.

Her long blond hair still matted from sleep was shoved under a silver gray fox hat. At six feet tall she made an impressive sight, especially after donning her bear skin coat. Next, twin 45 Colts were strapped around ample but shapely firm hips. Outside she tied on her snow shoes in preparation to walk her ten mile trap line. Steel blue eyes scanned the horizon for possible threat. Seeing none she headed out.

Back home in Cambridge she had been a school teacher, but longed for adventure. It was the 1850s and all ready corruption abounded. Judges made laws that made it hard to live. Politicians were always raising taxes. What was once referred to as the frontier was quickly becoming like the big cities back East. Greedy merchants charged far more for their merchandise than it was worth. Sally longed for the freedom she was promised when she first came here.

Sally was extremely attractive, but men shunned her because of her size. Lonely and frustrated she decided to head west, live or die, it had to be better. That's how she received the nickname Crazy Sally. A woman had to be crazy to live in the wilderness alone.

The wilderness fulfilled Sally's expectations and then some, all except for one. Even out here, men were intimidated by her strength and her height. Most were just drunken bums. After a few years in the wilderness she found her adventure, her freedom, but not her man.

It wasn't until she was half way through her trap line she heard it, a snort then the sound of a horse, no two horses sloshing through the snow. Then she saw him. A big man, six feet five at least, trail worn, experienced, dressed similar to she, but different. Not from this area, perhaps from farther north, Canada maybe. Never the less a true mountain man. Facial scars attested to an encounter with a grizzly, perhaps the very one that now served as a covering for his massive frame. His reddish- gray beard was long; even more reddish -gray hair braided Indian style hung beneath a beaver hat. His face was weathered indicating years in the high country, yet, even from this distance Sally detected his demeanor was one of calm assurance, someone who has experienced it all and conquered it all. The very type of man she had been looking for- one that could make her feel like a woman.

"Ya keep gawking like that and your face will freeze off." Shocked she didn't realize he had seen her, let alone only a few feet from her. Without waiting for a answer the stranger spoke.

"You must be the one they call crazy Sally."

"Yes I am, and who might I be talking to?"

"The name is Smith, Johnathan Smith, but most call me Grizz. Them your traps I spotted up the trail?"

"Yes they are." "No need to go any farther, they were empty. Don't suppose you would be a-mind to head back to your place? Could really use a meal made by a woman for a change. Don't worry I'm harmless."

Harmless as a grizzly she thought. But she was more intrigued

168   THE WILLS CREEK CHRONICLES

than scared. He didn't talk like most. She noticed by his speech he had had some education. Rare out here in the wilderness. The sun was setting by the time they arrived.

"You can put your horses in the lean to, I'll get the stove stoked up and start supper."

"Sounds good to me, Miss Sally." Miss Sally, she hadn't heard that in a long time. It sounded kind of nice for a change. The stove was soon hot and a pot of melted snow began to boil, four large pork chops sizzled in bear fat in the iron skillet. She was filling the pot with wild onions, carrots and potatoes from cold storage when Grizz walked through the door.

"What took you so long?"

"Just wanted to give you some time to think this over, out here all alone, you might have changed your mind and come out waving a scatter gun at me." I smelled the food cooking so I figured it would be okay to come in." Now Sally was really intrigued. The man had manners. Surely he was a man that feared little. But around her he seemed gentle as a lamb.

"You're in luck, butchered my last pig this fall, I don't suppose you would mind a few pork chops for supper?"

"Pork chops. I haven't had pork chops in years, not since I left Harvard."

"Harvard? you went to Harvard?

"Well I didn't actuality go there, I was a professor."

Thud.

"Sally, Sally, you all right?"

She woke up to this grizzly of a man sitting on the floor with her cradled in his arms, concerned about her well being. It felt good.

"Welcome back. Thought I'd lost you there for a minute. Be a shame to since I have traveled all this way to meet you."

"What? You purposely came down from the high mountains to meet me?" How did you know I even existed?"

"Shucks ma'am, your famous up there. I have been hearing about the blond school teacher that lived in the wilderness like a man for over a year." I figured I'd better hunt you up before you disappeared. There is only two things I've missed since coming out here, one a good home -cooked meal and the other to talk to someone who had some intelligence.

"Is that all you've missed?"

"Well there might be a third."

Sally couldn't believe her eyes , she actually saw him blush. Johnathan Smith wound up staying for more than supper, in fact he and Sally tripled the amount of traps that winter. All the time Grizz was a perfect gentleman. Sally was beginning to worry, she had fallen head over heels in love with this mountain man. But he never made a move. Then in the middle of March Grizz suggested they pack up the furs and head to St. Louis to trade them in. Sally for the first time became enraged. "Is that it," she screamed. "All I am to you was a trapping partner?" Sally broke down in tears.

"Sally my love, don't cry. Of course there is more you aren't any backwoods floozy, you're the one I love. I want to do this right. As soon as we reach St. Louis we're going to find us a preacher and get married."

"Married? You really want to marry me?

"Of course, then we'll come back here and raise us a bunch of little mountain boys and girls."

LINDA WARRICK

ONE SPECIAL FRIEND
Who Says A Man And Woman Can't Be "Just" Friends?

Seeing them turn red with obvious embarrassment was quite amusing to Matt, the one guy in the sophomore class most of the girls avoided. His favorite pastime was to grab their purses and spill personal items out over the top of a desk, or worse yet, if they happened to be at their locker, in the corridor.

How mortifying to have to scramble to pick up the contents before they were either trampled or anyone passing by saw every personal item it contained. His way of teasing girls was not only worse than annoying, but downright childish for a young man nearing 18 years of age. After one of Matt's usual escapades, Carrie Ann was especially frustrated and near tears. Why did he insist on picking on her? Her eyes caught classmate, Steven's as he stooped to help gather her possessions. Realizing he was one of the few guys that actually gave Matt the time of day, yet could tactfully put him in his place, she gratefully accepted his assistance.

The school year was rapidly drawing to a close and the faculty had arranged for their class to have a final field trip to Seneca Lake. The lake is at the head of Wills Creek and the tributaries that flow from it. Being May, it was still to cool to swim, but it was a beautiful day to picnic, play games or soak up some sun. As the class scattered to multiple areas of the park to pursue different interests, Steven approached Carrie Ann.

"Would you like to go for a walk? It's a really nice day," he commented. "Yeah, sure," she replied. "Anyway, I need to thank you for coming to my defense with Matt last week. He is so annoying. I just don't understand how you can even be friends with him."

Steven was quick to respond, "Oh, Matt was just being stupid. He doesn't know of any other way to get your attention. And unfortunately, he doesn't always think before he acts."

They strolled along the paved lanes of the park and came upon some swing sets and other outdoor equipment. There they spent several hours sitting on the swings conversing and sharing memories of their childhoods. She was drawn to his kind and understanding nature, so there grew an overwhelming mutual desire to become better acquainted.

Petite with wavy chestnut shoulder-length hair and big dark eyes Carrie Ann was an intelligent, but shy and quiet young lady. She was flattered that a guy was taking the time to get to know her, unlike most others she had met. The eldest of four children, she had been raised by strict parents and was somewhat naïve in the ways of society. Her parents had taken great pains to protect their children from the evils of the world. Tall and lanky with dark hair and hazel eyes, Steve was stately with his average looks.

But it was the humble and tender quality about him that made it impossible for her not to be drawn to him. Not to mention his quick wit. His father had died unexpectedly of heart failure when he was just 12, and it had obviously taken a toll on him. The youngest of three children, his much older brother and sister lived away from the area. Shy and somewhat insecure, he needed someone besides his loving, but highly protective mother, to care enough to make a difference in his life.

So Carrie and Steve built their relationship, first based on honesty and friendship. Here were two teenagers, insecure with themselves, searching for their identities and the meaning of life. A unique bond of trust had been built that enabled them to share their innermost thoughts and feelings. Together, they learned what unconditional love was. It developed into a beautiful friendship built on mutual respect.

They choose to limit their intimacy so as not to jeopardize their future. The plan was to marry in due time, so many hours were spent dreaming and charting their course of action for the years ahead. It was a foundation that made them each others best friend.

However, life eventually got in the way. Upon graduation from high school, circumstances lead them down two different paths. Steve enrolled in a school that moved him to Columbus, while Carrie Ann stayed in the area, and took a job. Eventually she met and married someone else and raised three children. Steve joined the Air Force and married a girl in England. He retired from a career in military intelligence and accepted a position as a special agent for the government. They had two sons and eventually settled in California.

While it is true that Steve and Carrie will always have a special bond based on the trusting and caring relationship they had in their youth, it is now one of a brother/sister kinship. Both will always cherish the days when they were each others best friend. They still are "just friends."

DONNA J. LAKE SHAFER

Uncle Jim Takes The Plunge
Comedy At The Family Reunion

Everyone was in a festive mood, laughing and teasing. That years family reunion was held at Auntie Marie and Uncle Joe's farm. There were twenty-seven grandchildren present, many aunts and uncles and of course, Grandma and Grandpa. The adults brought each other up to date on family happenings…who was born, who died and the concern over some of today's teenagers who seemed to be going down a path to destruction.

The many voices echoed great concern over the length of time the depression was likely to last. Then there was the reminiscing about the "good old days" when life was slower and the kids better behaved.

Sagging planks spanned saw-horses which bore platters of meats, greens, and hot casseroles. There were freshly baked pies and cakes plus sweating pitchers of iced lemonade. Newly churned butter on straight-from-the-oven rolls melted in the heat. An ancient oak formed a canopy over the feast.

Horseshoes, softball and tag were part of the activities of the day. Someone hitched up Ol' Bess, the family plow horse, and the city kids took turns riding her.

Someone called "swimming hole." Oh, happy thought! A swim in the cool waters of Rough'n'Ready, the Wills Creek tributary which made its way through the farm. As the young ones ran off, someone noted that Uncle Jim was tagging along. Everyone knew that Jim was deathly afraid of water. He would pick up a black snake with his bare hands, gentle an ornery horse or outstare a skunk. But when it came to water, well, that was a different story.

After much teasing and cajoling Jim agreed to wade along the shore. Being a tenderfoot, he pulled a pair of four buckle Artics from the rumble seat of the Model-A, stripped off his trousers and reluctantly headed for the dreaded water. Jim was of so-so height, a rather slightly built fella, and his boxer shorts skimmed the tops of his knobby knees. Quite a sight. Gingerly, he stepped into the creek. The gentle flow of the water and a certain firmness beneath the boots gave him a little confidence. It wasn't long 'til Jim, now feeling as sure-footed as a mountain goat, edged away from shore just a tad. Well now, that wasn't so bad so a little farther should be O.K., Jim thought. Suddenly, he was gone from sight.

Soon, erupting from the rousing waters were two rubber boots followed by skinny white legs, only to disappear again. A head appeared that spit and spluttered, and then arms that flailed about wildly. The curious sight emerged from the water and sloshed up the bank, red faced, soaked and muttering obscenities. Everyone cheered and agreed that Uncle Jim wasn't much of a swimmer but had indeed bravely faced his most dreaded adversary.

Aunt Tillie, Jim's adoring wife, swore that he never again took a bath in more than three inches of water. Maybe he did and maybe he didn't, but none of us ever saw him go near that swimming hole after that day. In fact, it was said that he never again mentioned that swimming hole. Not that one or any other one, not even once.

LINDA BURRIS

TALE OF TWO WEDDINGS
Love Is In The Air On A Summer Day

Today is our daughter Susan's wedding. She's 21 and will be married on this beautiful summer day. Birds are singing among the trees in our backyard, a luscious green carpet of grass. The sky is bright blue with fluffy white clouds. Wills Creek is bubbling its way toward our small town in Southeastern Ohio.

The lawn will soon be full with tables and chairs, a white arch bedecked with pink and white flowers and greenery. There will be a white canopy set up for the tables laden with food, and a four-tiered wedding cake, iced white with pink trim.

This day reminds me of my wedding in a small church in my hometown in February 1970. It was sunny, the sky bright blue, white floating clouds and the temperature in the 50's. We held the wedding in the church sanctuary and the reception in the basement.

Susan will be dressed in a floor-length gown with chapel train and a white lace Belgium veil. Her bouquet will include pink and white roses and trimmed with lace. There will be smaller versions for the flower girl, maid of honor, and four bridesmaids.

The groom, Sam, the ring bearer and his groomsmen will wear white tuxedos with tails, white top hats, white long-sleeved shirts and white shoes. The boutonnieres will be pink carnations. The bridesmaids wear pink ankle-length dresses, white gloves and pink shoes.

In my wedding there was only one maid of honor, my sister Janet, and Ed Hockenberry was the best man. The men wore suits with a white carnation on their suits lapels. Janet wore a light, blue formal gown with a lace veil and white shoes. She carried a bouquet of blue and white carnations trimmed with lace. Long white, floor-length gown and veil, white shoes and bouquet of blue and white carnations completed my wedding attire.

Today the wedding music will be played by a string quartet. There will be singing by Susan's sister, Julie, before and during the wedding. The couple wrote their own vows. Rev. Walsh will conduct the lighting of the Unity Candle and the ring exchange ceremony, then pronounce them man and wife. The wedding will end with the couple's kiss, after which they will exit to the receiving line for best wishes from those in attendance and reception at the Elks Lodge.

Our wedding was performed by Rev. Willis. The music was played by the church organist. My father escorted me down the aisle and gave me away. We repeated our wedding vows, exchanged rings, were pronounced man and wife , kissed and walked to the rear of the church to shake hands and thank those who attended. All of these memories remind me of those days of yesteryear. Sadness creeps inside me as I realize my sweet Susie's wedding will begin a new phase of her life and mine.

JOETTA VARANASI

Neighborhood Excitement
Missing For Hours...Then Screams From The Creek

A police officer stood at the door holding a picture of a young girl. "We have an Amber Alert in this neighborhood. Has anyone seen this child today?" he spoke sternly in a deep voice. "Her name is Pam Jones. She lives across the street."

Carolyn stood in her doorway looking at the picture. "I know her," she said. "I saw her this morning in her front yard. How long has she been missing?"

Since around noon" he replied. "Her mom looked out the window at 11:45 a.m. and she was in her sandbox. At noon she called Pam for lunch, but she was gone."

Carolyn was unable to offer any more information.

The officer explained, "Pam's mother thought she might have gone to a neighbor's house, but after making a phone call and finding out she didn't, Mrs. Jones immediately called the police department to report her missing. It's been four hours since she was last seen and there are only a few more hours of daylight. We don't have much time."

"What can we do to help? Carolyn asked, seeing neighbors already posting Pam's picture on trees and telephone poles along the street.

"Pam's puppy was with her this morning." "We haven't had a report on a dog." The officer said, a surprised look on his face. "I'll talk to her mom."

When Pam wasn't in daycare and the weather was nice, she loved playing outdoors with her puppy Spot. With the excitement of Pam's disappearance, no one noticed that Spot was missing also. After speaking with Mrs. Jones, the officer learned that Spot hadn't been seen for hours. She told police that Pam's puppy usually took a nap on the front yard in the sun or on the back porch if it was raining. It had been a bright sunny day, but now the wind was blowing in dark clouds.

Police suspected that Pam and her puppy were together somewhere. But where?

Emergency vehicles were parked all over the neighborhood. Neighbors walked through the backyards looking for Pam and her puppy as the cumulus clouds made the dusk ominous. The search was finally called off until morning.

Shortly after dark, screams were heard from behind the Jones home, drifting up from the banks of Wills Creek. "Mommy, Mommy," the child's voice repeated frantically. "I'm lost. Get me out of here!" The distressed voice came from some distance away.

The family ran to the back door while Pam's brother dialed 911. Emergency workers arrived almost immediately to begin cutting through the heavy brush and debris along the creek.

When they finally reached the terrified Pam, Spot was by her side. She said in a soft, relieved voice. "I want my mommy!"

"We'll have you back to your mommy in a few minutes," said a rescue worker, gently holding her hand.

Back at the house, Pam told the large crowd of neighbors that she followed Spot down the hill and couldn't find her way back. She and Spot laid down on the banks of Wills Creek and had a long nap in the sun. Upon awakening, Pam said, they picked wild flowers and ran along the creek banks until it got dark. Spot led her back to where they first napped, but they remained lost until the rescue workers found them.

The entire neighborhood, sharing a feeling of relief, enjoyed a good night's sleep knowing that Pam and her puppy were now safe at home.

JANET MONTE

Life Changes Forever
Present And Future

The phone rang shrilly, jolting Sandy awake. Looking at the clock. It's 6 a.m. She groans. This had better be good.

Jessica apologizes for waking her. " I wouldn't call Mom, but I need help. I can't find anyone to pick up the kids at five. Chad doesn't get home till 5:30. I have to work over today.

As Sandy slides out of bed and agrees to pick them up. She has hardly slept four hours.

Heading for a shower, she decides she will go to work early. That way she can leave early. As she leaves the house at 7:30 a.m., she wishes she could get one good night's sleep. Taking sleeping pills every night is not working. Seems like forever since she got good quality sleep. The pills only work for a few hours now.

Her head is splitting and it is only noon. Taking two aspirins, she hears the phone ringing loudly. It is not even 9 a.m.. One thing about it, this job is not slowing down with the recession. Everyone needs some form of insurance.

The clock strikes four, time to leave work and run errands, pick up the grand kids, and drop them off with their dad. She heads for home. Bumper to bumper traffic. She knows supper won't be until 6:30 or 7 again tonight. It is times like this that she hates living in the big city.

Arriving home, Sandy sees Keith's car in the garage. Hope he has started supper. I'm really beat. I just want to sleep. Smelling food cooking, she knows supper is on. I love this man; he tries to help me so much without being asked. Maybe I can get to bed early.

After supper, Keith suggests she take a hot tub bath, two Tylenol and turn off the bedroom phone, and try to get some sleep. Maybe the warm soak will do the trick. Great idea. he will take all calls.

Sandy pulls the drapes to darken the room and climbs into bed. Turns on the TV and goes right to sleep. Two hours later wide awake. Keith is sound asleep beside her, snoring loudly.

Getting up and trying the other bedroom, she finds after tossing and turning for a hour, this is not working. Since sleep isn't happening, she will make her list of things that need done.. But coffee first.

Keith gets up at 7:30, comes walking out and sees that it was not a good night again. He decides not to ask about the strong coffee.

At 8:30 a.m. Sandy calls her sister, Jill, and tells her about her night. "I can't stay asleep long. I have no energy and I drag through the day. I've got to do something," she said..

After listening for a half hour, Jill suggests a sleep test. See what the doctor can find. "Maybe you have sleep apnea," she offers.

At 9 a.m. Sandy calls Dr. Sean, who agrees she needs testing for a start. He has a cancellation. Be at the clinic at 7:30 p.m.

At the clinic, a nurse tells Sandy the procedure, shows her the bedroom setting and tells her to do what she would normally do at home when going to bed. Sandy showers, takes two Tylenol, and turns on the TV. The nurses hook her up to machine. Two hours later Sandy is wide awake and finds the nurse has turned off the TV. Turning the TV back on, she dozes off and on for the rest of night.

At 5:30 a.m., she leaves clinic. The doctor will call her later with the results. Heading home she feels like she has not slept forever. They have got to find something soon or she will be dead from lack of sleep, if that is possible. She believes it is possible.

Dr. Sean calls at 10 a.m. to say she does not have sleep apnea, but the testing did show she has a sleeping problem. He thinks they need to reprogram her body. Says she will need two weeks off work to go somewhere quit to relax. He will give her instructions.

Sandy tells Keith what the doctor wants to try. Keith advises Sandy to go for it. What have you got to lose?

Sandy calls Jill, tells her what she has to do. Jill says, "Fine. I know of a bed & breakfast in the country that would be the perfect place. Jill books two weeks for Sandy.

Sandy heads to Northeastern Ohio; Keith is handling things at home. He tells her to just relax. If an emergency comes up, he will let her know. She's to ID her calls, and only answer his calls. He will call each night to say goodnight.

Arriving Hill Top that afternoon, Jill meets Sandy to introduce her to Susannah. She owns the B&B, a beautiful Victorian home with a large wrap-around porch. She is shown her suite – French looking with lace curtains on all the windows, lots of antique furniture and a canopy bed. Sandy tells Susannah she needs a dark room; these curtains won't work. But out of sight are room-darkening shades at top of the windows. Very hidden.

Jill and Sandy head out to spend some time sightseeing and eat at an Amish restaurant. Arriving back at Hill Top at 8 p.m., they sit on the porch to chat with other guests. Later, with the night sounds and no cars or sirens, Sandy wonders if she will ever get to sleep. Wait a minute... she did not see a TV in her room. Now what is she going to do?

She takes out the instructions from Dr. Sean, and finds some sleeping pills and a CD, which she places in the player. The first part is on relaxing and breathing techniques. The next part is on the sleeping pills, to which very soon you will not need. They are just to help you now with the process.

The CD includes water sounds with soft music and bird sounds in the background. Six hours later she awakens to find that she had slept six peaceful hours. Looking outside she decides since it is still dark, she will try the process again to get back to sleep. If that doesn't she will read a book until breakfast.

Its 7 a.m. Sandy awakens and can't believe how good she feels. This is a first. She hopes this keeps up forever. It is like being reborn. She will meet Jill later. Heading for breakfast she asks Susannah for a map and directions to Salt Fork Lake. They are going boat riding and get some sun and relax... and talk all day.

On the way to the lake, she calls Keith to tell him of her first night and how great she feels. Hopefully this will work forever. She is praying anyway and will keep doing what Dr. Sean tells her. Keith says this is the best news in a long time. She sounds so happy.

Driving secondary roads, she rolls down the windows to feel the breeze and smell the country air. Birds are singing and there is wind in the trees. Crossing a creek she stops to watch deer drinking. She realizes how beautiful the wild flowers are and everything is so green. She spots some butterflies. All at once Sandy is feeling peaceful.

Jill, waiting at the dock, tells Sandy how restful she looks. Dr. Sean's book must work. When Sandy tells her about the deer, Jill notes that she had crossed Wills Creek, which winds through several counties, with lots of wildlife using it And the fishing is good there. Maybe we will try that.

Sandy can't believe she has been here for one week already. I feel so rested, and tonight I am going to try not taking a sleeping pill. See if just the relaxing technique will work. Next morning, Sandy tells Susannah her it took a few times of playing the CD and telling herself to relax, but in no time she was asleep and slept the night away.

Boy! Will Dr. Sean be proud of me. This really works...and no TV in the bedroom. I would of never have thought I could sleep without it. The noise used help to drown out the other sounds. Wait until I tell Keith no TV ever again in our bedroom. Dr. Sean said the bedroom is for sleeping and we have to train our body for sleep. Maybe a few other activities. Ha.

ABOUT THE AUTHORS

JOY L. WILBERT ERSKINE writes short stories, usually about relationships. She pens silly poems for fun and loves to write occasional guest columns for *The Daily Jeffersonian* in Cambridge. Avid interests in travel, genealogy, needle arts, and all things Celtic keep her happy at home and active in the community.

LINDA BURRIS likes to spend time with her family in addition to writing. She bowls with four teammates.. Her favorite reading is historical novels, suspense novels and books about the Amish. She writes short stories for adults and children as well as Christian poetry.

BARBARA KERNODLE-ALLEN grew up in the oil fields of Ohio, W.Va. and Michigan. She put down roots near family in Cambridge in the 1970's. An activity therapist at Cambridge Psychiatric Hospital until retirement, her interests include family, cooking, genealogy, the cat, games, and learning to write fiction.

SAMUEL D. BESKET is a graduate of Cambridge High School. He served four years in the U.S. Air Force during the Vietnam War before starting a career at Champion Spark Plug which spanned four decades. He is an avid reader, a guest columnist in *The Daily Jeffersonian*, and enjoys short story writing.

MARILYN DURR writes in several genres, including fiction and non-fiction. She owned and published The Contractor's Marketplace advertising media while living in Indiana. Her Halloween column and a guest column was published in *The Daily Jeffersonian*. Her interests lean toward writing, reading, cooking, and crafts.

RICHARD A. DAIR was originally a wildlife artist, Rick has now expanded into writing short stories depicting the outdoors. A history buff, his stories depict mountain men, early American life, and western themes.

JOETTA VARANASI writes poetry and short stories. Though much of her work captures life in a steel town, her chapbooks depict snow in New England, train travel, coal fields, and a vista of Wills Creek from her picture window. She is a graduate of Ohio University and lives in Norman Plaza.

BEVERLY JUSTICE is a Kent State graduate and life-long resident of Cambridge. She enjoys writing short stories and traditional poetry. She is a member of the Daughters of Union Veterans and the Southeastern Ohio Civil War Roundtable. Bev shares her home with six rescued cats.

MARALYN COOPER O'CONNELL is a retired RN, artist, avid crafter, gardener, and animal lover. She has always been fond of limericks and enjoys writing them.

DONNA J. LAKE SHAFER is married with children, grandchildren and great-grandchildren. A Cambridge native, she has lived in other cities and states but has always returned to these old hills. An avid reader with radio commercial experience, she has only recently turned to short story writing.

LINDA WARRICK enjoys writing on a variety of subjects, including life's interesting twists and turns, her passions for seaside travel, home/garden décor and design, as well as memory book-making. She currently writes the Heritage Quest column for *The Daily Jeffersonian* focusing on genealogy tips.

J. PAULETTE MEDLEY-CARTER FORSHEY is a lifetime resident of Guernsey County and award-winning writer and poet for 19 years. She's a member of Romance Writer's of America, Central Ohio Fiction Writers, and the Cambridge Writer's Workshop.

ABOUT THE AUTHORS 185

PAM RITCHEY makes her home in Kimbolton with her young grandson. She has written several articles on her family's genetic health problems for various publications. She also writes short stories, poems, young reader's chapter books and has a novel in progress. She was compiler and technical adviser for CWW's first book, "The Day We Learned to Write and Other Acts of Madness."

JANET MONTE has been a resident here since 1979. She moved her because of Salt Fork Lake and the beautiful rolling hills. She loves to read, travel and take photographs of her trips for her journals. She taught boating for five years. She enjoys cooking and do oil and watercolor paintings.

DONNA WELLS enjoys reading best-sellers and the classics. She likes all types of writing, especially stories with a happy conclusion. "The best part of writing is the research." says. Donna volunteers as a Dickens Ambassador at the Dickens Historic Village. She was a model for a life-like mannequin which will be stationed just outside the Dickens Welcome Center this Christmas.

DICK METHENY lived most of his life in Medina County. For the last eight years he has lived on a small farm near Quaker City. An avid reader, he also has his first novel nearly completed and has started second one. He's a charter member of CWW.

DONA McCONNELL spent 30 years as a corporate writer before turning to fiction. Favorite topics include relationships, character studies and Southern themes. In addition to writing, she has taught English at several colleges, including Marietta College. She is currently working on two books.

JERRY WOLFROM, CWW instructor, spent forty-six years in the newspaper business. He continues to write six humor columns a week as well as outdoor magazine articles, particularly fishing. He currently is writing his sixth book titled, "Dating For Geezers."

Made in the USA